Robotto, Otto

#1 A ROBOT

ESCAPES

Peter HenKal

the watermark press

Robotto, Otto #1 – A Robot EscApEs

© pEtER HEnKAl

First published in 2022
by The Watermark Press, Plettenberg Bay
All rights reserved.

Editing and project management by Mike Kantey
Design and layout by Sonja Kantey
Marketing By Evolution Media House

Printed by BKBookbinders, Durban

ISBN 978-1-7764288-3-0

For Michele

Thank you for your encouragement from start to finish.

MR PETER HENKAL

PRELUDE

The definition of a robot

A machine that resembles a living creature in being capable of moving independently (as by walking or rolling on wheels) and performing complex actions (such as grasping and moving objects). Already at the beginning of the 21st Century, robots are entering our homes as fully automated cleaning and cooking appliances. They are also becoming more human in the form of companion robots.

In the following narrative, I have tweaked my "hero" to represent a still higher level of self-learning.

NakaRobotto #15.20.20.15

Late afternoon in down-town Tokyo, Japan:

Getting closer to 6 p.m., the factory comes to a halt. Mr Watanabe Fumio, the lanky quality inspector, breathes an audible sigh of relief. Dressed in a much too large, white coat with soiled, white cotton gloves on his hands, he hefts the last robot off the conveyor belt.

Watanabe's daily production sheet reads as follows:

100 x Naka Robotto – Model 1500 M MediuM
Robot CoMpaNioN/HousekeepeR

Adjusting his thick spectacles on his rather long nose, he hastily opens the robot's breastplate to insert the fully charged battery. Next, he attaches a sticker which reads –

FiNal iNspeCtioN No:15.20.20.15

While replacing the breastplate, his gloved hand brushes against the robot's *ON/OFF* switch. Being in a hurry, however, the inspec- tor carries the 1.5-metre tall robot to the last open space on the bottom shelf of a long storage rack. On the following morning the robots will be boxed and stored in a warehouse.

A shrill bell announces the end of the shift. The lights are switched off one by one, the assembly line workers – mainly female – push through the door to the change rooms.

Given his important position as the quality inspector, Watanabe is responsible for locking up. On this day, he is in a great hurry to get out of the robot factory. Not bothering to have a final look around, he rushes after the others and forgets to lock the door. Silence then spreads throughout the factory building.

Naka Robotto No.15.20.20.15 slowly opens his eyes.

Where am I?

I look to my right, where the other robots are lined up.

Why do none of them have their eyes open?

Carefully I move, first my right arm, then my left arm; my left leg, my right leg –

All moving smoothly.

I step off the bottom shelf, onto the factory floor. At the very last moment, I totter and lose my balance, hold on to my neighbour: crash goes the entire bottom row of robots. One after the other, they topple and fall onto the hard factory floor.

Panicked, I look around: a sliver of light, falling through the glass-pane of the door, beckons me to the stairway. I look back to the others on the floor in horror.

Should I help the unbroken ones? Ask them to join me? None are moving a limb; eyes are all closed. Maybe several robots leaving the factory will attract attention; better that I go on my own, take a chance.

I move forward slowly, uncertain as to where to go. The stairwell leading to the other floors is lit up by small led lights.

Where must I go?

The noise of traffic is coming from below.

That must be the way out of the building.

Careful not to fall again, I hang on to the handrail, taking one step at a time. Through the closed glass doors of the ground-floor foyer, I can see people and cars rushing by. I have reached street level, but the glass door is closed, no sign of any handles.

How do they open?

Hurried footsteps are coming from the stairs above, *clip, clop, clip, clop,* getting louder, getting closer. I duck behind a small desk in the entrance foyer. It must be the receptionist's desk, who by now has also gone home. The footsteps rush past my hiding place to- wards the sliding glass doors. They *swoosh* open as the footsteps approach, Then I hear the doors *swoosh* shut again.

Will the doors open for me?

Only one way to find out: stomping my feet hard, I advance toward the doors – *swoosh* – they open. I step out, take a look, first left, then right. The people are rushing past me. Nobody is taking any notice of me.

> *Where can I go?*

Most people that come past turn into an arcade just a short walk away.

> *Let's go!*

CHAPTER ONE

The arcade is narrow, just wide enough for four people – maybe two one way, and two the opposite way. Narrow shops line the thoroughfare on either side – bookstores, clothing shops, a florist, take-away foods, it goes on and on.

Undecided where to go, I follow two young girls, about my height. In no hurry, they are taking their time in checking out different clothing boutiques. Careful not to attract attention to myself, I nearly bump into an A-framed signboard of a bakery, advertising today's specials.

"Hey, I like your outfit," says a bright-eyed bakery assistant, about my height. Wiping a strand of hair out of his face, he says: "Better than those stupid Spiderman or Superman outfits most kids wear nowadays."

Looking me up and down, he continues: "I am just about to walk up and down the passage with our special's board over my shoulders, would you do it for me? We are about the same height, but you attract much more attention than I, plus – to tell you the truth – I need the bathroom real bad. What do you say? I'll give you a couple of Yen."

Uncertain of my voice, I stammer: "Er, sure – why not?" Finding that the words come out more easily than I thought, I say: "If – if you think I – I can do – do it."

"Nothing to it," he says, "just walk up and down the arcade. If you get tired, you can come back to this shop. I'll lift the sign off your shoulders, OK?" Without waiting for a reply, he hefts the A-frame over my head and onto my shoulders. With my helmet barely sticking over the top of the A-frame, he asks: "Is that good for you?" I nod. If I take small steps, I figure that I'll be fine.

Maybe ten steps away from the bakery, a young couple stops in front of me to study the specials. "Oh look –" the girl says, "what a good idea to use a robot to carry this board! I felt so sorry for Kamin, humping that heavy board up and down. I suppose, as a casual assistant, he has to do what Mr. Yamashita tells him to do," she says to her boyfriend, who winks at me and taps me on the helmet. "Thanks for showing us the menu. Off you go. We know what we are going to order."

I walk back and forth, from one end of the arcade to the other, stopping for people that step in front of me to read the specials.

At 9.30 p.m. the bakery assistant (who the girl had called "Kamin") is waiting for me in the door of the shop. "Hey, aren't you tired yet? You never stopped. Come, let me take that A-frame off you. I am done for today. I only work from 4.30 to 9.30 p.m., Wednesdays to Fridays, to make some extra money for a new laptop. My present one is a hand-down from my father, much too old, and the graphics suck," he says, handing me 100 yen (roughly one US dollar).

"Kamin, you can keep your money. I don't need money at all," I tell him.

"What do you mean, you don't need money? Are you a rich kid posing in this fancy outfit?" he asks, but then he takes a closer look. "This is not a fancy-dress outfit: are you a real Robot? He points at the inspection label, stuck to my chest: "Naka Robotto No.15.20.20.15.

"Wow! You're not kidding! Who do you belong to?" Kamin asks.

"Nobody," I say, "I was running away from the factory down the road when you stopped me."

"So where are you going to go? Where will you sleep?" asks Kamin, deep concern visible in his face. Then he brightens. "Do you want to come home with me?" he asks, "at least until we figure out what to do?" he asks.

"If it's no trouble for you," I reply, relieved to have found a place to hide for the night.

CHAPTER TWO

On their way to the boy's home, he doesn't stop talking for a second.

"I stay with my parents, not even ten minutes' walk from here," he babbles. "I'm an only child, surname Gushiken and we're originally from Okinawa. My father's given name is Akio. He's a computer programmer in an IT company and my mother's given name is Keiko, she is a beautician in the Isetan Department Store. I'm in my last year of Junior High School, JHS3; next April, I will go to high school. My father wants me to become a Computer programmer as well and I would like that very much. Right, here we are: our apartment is on the fourth floor; we can take the elevator."

After Kamin pulls me into the small cubicle I take a slow look around because by now I am a little bit confused. But when the elevator shakes and rumbles as it begins its ascent, I grab hold of Kamin's arm in horror.

"It's all right," he says, "calm down. Nothing is going to happen to us. We're just going up in the elevator."

"Hello, Kamin, is this one of your school friends, dressed in the latest robot fashion?" asks a surprised Mr Gushiken when the two of us enter the living room.

"No father," Kamin says, "he is not a school friend – he is an escaped robot."

The boy's parents listen very carefully to the full story, but Mrs Gushiken is not happy. "You must take him back to the factory tomorrow, before school," she says," they will miss him."

"No!" I protest, "I am not going back there. I want to pick my own home. If you do not like me, I can go and find another home tomorrow."

"Now wait a minute," interrupts Mr Gushiken, "don't get us wrong. We are not saying we don't like you, it's just not right that we keep you, knowing very well who you still belong to."

"Why can't we go and buy him?" asks Kamin.

Mr and Mrs Gushiken look at one another for a long time, before they finally nod to each other.

"Kamin," says Mrs Gushiken, "we have felt a little guilty for leaving you on your own since I started work again. You seemed to be all right on your own, with your homework, your laptop and your job at the bakery. Do you think that maybe a friend would be something good to have around?"

Kamin now breaks into a big smile, "Oh yes, Mom! I'll help pay for him with my bakery money."

"What about your new laptop?" his father asks.

"That can wait, Dad. Right now I'll have no time for stupid games. Now I have the real thing."

Much to their surprise I say: "I can help around the apartment, too. As a so-called 'companion robot', I have been programmed to do all the housework. I can also help Kamin at the bakery with the SpeCial's board and make sure he does his homework."

"Well, that all sounds very exciting," says Mr Gushiken. Let's talk to the owner of the factory tomorrow. Meanwhile we'll need to find a name for you. Let me have a look at those final inspection certificate numbers."

As a software programmer, Mr Gushiken is used to thinking in numbers, algorithms, and mathematical equations. "Naka Robotto No: 15.20.20.15 – wait, let me think … The 15th letter in the alphabet is the letter 'O'; the 20th is 'T', followed by another 20, which means another 'T', and then another 15 makes for another 'O'.

"So, we have: 'O-T-T-O'; his given name will have to be 'Otto'," he says, holding up the equation triumphantly.

Kamin immediately high-fives his father. "Dad, you are a genius!"

"My name is Robotto, Otto," I say, laughing out loud with pride. They all join in, laughing at him dancing in the middle of the living room: "Robotto, Otto – Robotto, Otto …"

"That is a very nice given name," says Mrs Gushiken finally when I am getting dizzy. "Otto, pronounced 'Ah-to' in Japanese means *wealthy, rich.*"

"We are going to get RICH!" laughs Kamin, throwing his arms

around me in a tight embrace. Mr and Mrs Gushiken smile at each other, nodding again.

CHAPTER THREE

Punctual as always at 7.00 a.m., Fumio Watanabe feels for the department door keys in the pocket of his white dustcoat, before inserting one in the keyhole to find the door already unlocked.

Did I forget to lock up in my haste? he chides himself, *that was really careless.*

Pushing the door fully open, he rounds the corner onto the factory floor and catches his breath.

What on earth is going on here?

The entire bottom row of robots has fallen off the storage-rack and is lying in a heap on the hard floor.

As the continually arriving assembly-line workers push past him, however, he jumps into action.

"You, you and you, clean up this mess!" he orders. "Take these pieces to the repair shop for salvage. Hurry, hurry! The conveyor belt is about to start with today's production."

His workers obey immediately, speculating quietly among themselves about the possible cause of the disaster.

"Lucky for us," one says, "it's not our fault; otherwise we would have lost our pay."

Minutes later the conveyor belt starts moving and another working day has begun.

Half an hour later Mrs Gushiken, attractively dressed and exquisitely made-up for her job as a beautician, passes through the automatic sliding doors of the Advanced Intelligence Robotics (AIR) factory building. Approaching the smiling receptionist, she asks to see the owner on a matter of great importance. Less than two minutes later, she stands opposite the elderly, white-haired proprietor Mr Shushumi Suzuki.

"Good morning, sir," Mrs Gushiken says softly, "I am sorry to intrude on you so early without an appointment, but I have a matter of great concern to discuss with you."

Smoothing his long white hair, Mr Suzuki points to a chair opposite him and looks expectantly at her. She tells him the whole story; going into great detail about how her son and the robot had become acquainted and how he had offered to work off the amount owing. After listening intently to her story with a grave face, Mr Suzuki instructs his secretary to send for the quality inspector.

When the man appears before him, nervously clasping and unclasping his gloved hands, Mr Suzuki asks with a stern face: "Are you missing a Naka Robotto this morning?"

Not wanting to admit that he had not locked the door to his department the night before, the Inspector says defensively: "Sir, we made 100 robots yesterday, as we do every day. Nevertheless, I must have been careless in stacking the last row. When I opened up this morning, one entire row of robots had fallen off the storage rack onto the factory floor. The repair shop just told me they had to scrap some of them, the limb functions were damaged beyond repair."

"Accidents happen," says the elderly owner. "Please make sure you file an insurance claim." With that, he dismisses the quality inspector; turns to his guest, and with a wry little smile says: "If he says nothing is missing, then you can't have one of our robots, can you now? He must have run away from someone else. Shall we leave it at that?"

"If you are sure, thank you very much, Mr Suzuki. Have a nice day." says Mrs Gushiken, shaking the smiling factory owner's hand.

Upstairs, on the factory floor, where the conveyor had to be stopped in his absence, and overtime would have to be worked in to reach their daily target, a highly annoyed Watanabe, Fumio swears that – no matter what it takes – he will get the robot that caused him so much embarrassment. He could have lost his job.

CHAPTER FOUR

Back in the Gushiken apartment, unaware of the developments taking place at the AIR factory, I ask Kamin to show me where his mother keeps all the cleaning stuff.

"Some is over there in the passage cupboard; the rest you will find in the cupboard under the kitchen sink," says the boy, skipping to the door, school satchel over his shoulder, "See you later, have fun, bye."

"Hey, wait!" I stop him, "before you go, help me make up the futon beds. I can't reach all the way across."

"I am late already," Kamin replies, "can't we do it later?"

"No way, come on," I protest and of course I am right, because with one of us on each side of the futon, we are done in no time at all.

"See you later, bye," and Kamin is gone.

Like all the other robots of this series, I am programmed to do housework. It is a big selling point for this new range of the model 1500 Robots: they are multi-talented, useful companions. On my first day in my new home, I begin by having a good look around. In Tokyo they say that space is at a premium and accommodation is therefore both restricted and expensive. This small apartment must be typical, I suppose, with an open- plan living-room and kitchen; a larger bedroom for Mr and Mrs Gushiken and a smaller room for Kamin; one bathroom, with toilet and shower; and a passage with several cupboards. That's it – small, but airy and adequate.

I do the dusting first, wiping all the furniture; then wash the dirty breakfast dishes; sweep and mop the hard-wood floors.

Nothing to it! Now what? I still have time. Let me clean the glass-shower enclosure and the mirrors.

For that I need something to stand on and in the passage cupboard I find a three-step, fold-up ladder.

Perfect.

At 2.15 p.m. Kamin opens the apartment door, "Wow, look at that," he says, "the whole place is sparkling, and even smells good. You sure know how to clean. Wait until my parents see this."

"I hope they are happy with me, I really want to stay here," I reply.

"Sure, you'll see, all will be OK. Mother is going to pay for you, and we pay her back." says Kamin.

I wonder how much that will be.

For the next hour I look over Kamin's shoulder, checking his homework. "Up to what level in schooling have you been programmed?" asks Kamin, in awe at my knowledge.

"I don't know," I say, confused by the boy's question.

"Don't worry, my father can plug you into his computer and check your programme. Come, let's go to the bakery," says Kamin, closing the last of his books.

CHAPTER FIVE

The narrow bakery, situated in an equally narrow arcade belongs to Mr & Mrs Yamashita, a hard-working, yet jolly couple in their 50s. He bakes and she serves from behind the counter. During the late afternoons and evenings, the small bakery gets really busy, since most Japanese people have something to eat on their way home, and it is at this time that Kamin's help is required. On this day, he pulls me into the shop with him.

"Ah there you are!" says the baker, wiping his floury hands on his apron, while smiling at me. "You carried the special's board yesterday, didn't you? Some of our regular customers have complimented us on having a robot carry the A-frame, instead of the boy. Besides, you attracted a lot of attention. Can you work every afternoon when Kamin works?"

"Yes, I can do that," I say, "but what is the pay? We have to pay off my price at the factory.

"I see …" Mr Yamashita rubs his chin. "Well, in that case," he says, "I will pay you 500 yen for the afternoon."

"Great! My name is Robotto, Otto, but please call me 'Ah-to'." I bow politely to the baker, before turning to Kamin beside me. "Please help me lift the special's board, I want to get going."

Today, I am not as nervous as the day before; in fact, I am relieved and very happy with my life away from the factory, no longer scared or uncertain. I am confident it will all work out well for me.

I walk, and I walk – stopping for shoppers to read the board. Soon I realise that passers-by do not realise that I can talk. They think I am just a mechanical robot, shuffling up and down.

I will read the specials out to them.

"Try Today's Tasty Bakery Specials," I announce in my clear, young boy's voice. Two teenage boys stop me to have a look.

"Hi, you look hungry," I say, to their amazement.

"How do you know?" asks the boy with a bright-red baseball cap pulled low over his eyes, squinting at me.

"I can hear your stomach rumble from here," I smile. They snigger and nudge each other.

"He's cool," says the redcap boy. "Yes, you are right, we are hungry. Let's get some cookies – see you!" and they are on their way to the bakery.

"Try our tasty treats …" I say, and on and on I walk.

After maybe one hour, the arcade is packed with people. Having just passed the door to the baker, I hear desperate shouts from behind me.

"Stop him, stop him, stop the thief! He stole my bag! Stop him!" As I turn to see what is going on behind me; I get knocked down by a wild-eyed youngster who is in such a mad rush to leave the arcade that he does not see me and my A-frame. The bag he has just snatched flies out of his hands in the collision, the thief gets entangled with me and my heavy A-frame and starts kicking me to free himself.

Kamin, who has come out of the shop to see what is going on, barely sees the handbag flying toward him, when his goal-keeping instincts take over. Jumping forward, he gets hold of the bag, clutching it to his chest as if it were a football, and promptly falls on top of me. All of us are stuck in the A-frame with the thief screaming in agony, trapped below both of us.

Loud shouts echo through the arcade; women are screaming, lifting various small children to their chests, trying to get away. A group of older boys have realised what is happening, and rush forward to hold the thief down, while helping Kamin to his feet, still clutching the bag. Then they try to untangle me from my A-frame. Four girls, just leaving the boutique opposite the bakery, shriek and giggle at the pile of writhing bodies, but one stern glance from an elderly onlooker makes them blush with embarrassment. Then I hear the shrill whistle of a policeman, running towards the scene, where he opens up enough room to restore some form of order. Bending down, he handcuffs the thief, and hoists him to his feet. The older boys are still standing by with clinched fists, as if to say: "Try and run, see how far you will get!"

Minutes later, a police car stops at the entrance to the arcade, siren blaring. Two officers get out in order to disperse the staring crowd.

"Move on, move on, let us do our job," they bark.

Smart phones are hoisted on selfie-sticks, taking numerous flash shots of Kamin, the woman clutching her salvaged bag, the policeman with the cuffed youth, and me, the robot with the A-frame.

"Did you see how that robot tackled the thief?" one teenage boy asks his friend.

"Great job," he agrees.

The bystanders are now clapping and cheering when the youth is escorted to the waiting police car.

"Well done guys," says one of the teenagers, giving me what they say is a "high-five".

Right at the back of the assembled crowd stands the lanky body of Mr Watanabe, Fumio the quality inspector at AIR.

"Is that the robot that got away from me?" he mutters, pushing through the people in front of him. "Excuse me," he says, tapping Kamin on the shoulder, "is your surname Gushiken?" he asks.

"Yes," answers Kamin, "why are you asking?"

"Oh, just by coincidence I met, what must be, your mother today."

"I see," says Kamin, but before he has a chance to ask more details, Mrs Yamashita, the baker's wife, beckons for him to help her in the shop.

"Sorry, got to go!"

It takes another good half hour for things to return to normal; with many blocking the entrance to the bakery, to get a glimpse of Kamin and myself inside. The baker beckons to Kamin, showing him his smart phone: "Look at this: our pictures are on Facebook. We got over a thousand likes already."

The woman whose bag was stolen walks into the shop a short while later: "I don't know how to thank you two," she says.

"Money will do fine," says Mrs Yamashita drily, "they are both working here to earn extra pocket money."

The woman laughs: "Of course, I should have thought of that." She then digs in her purse, and hands me 2000 yen, "Share it between you."

"Thank you," I say, handing the money to Kamin, "we are saving for a new laptop."

"Are you? My husband is the pawnbroker further down the arcade; his shop gets many laptops that don't get claimed. Why don't we go and have a look right now, before he closes up for the night?" she says.

Kamin looks to the baker.

"Off you go, you two heroes," he beams. "Go claim your reward."

We catch up with the woman just outside the pawn shop, where she is telling her husband to wait for a moment. "I can't thank you enough; it all went so fast, I couldn't lock this shop fast enough to go after this thug," he says, shaking both our hands, a little more awkwardly with me. "You are looking for a laptop? Have a look on that shelf on the left. Youngsters come and pawn them, maybe to get money for drugs, I don't know, and never come back," he says.

Kamin spots a brand new-looking leather laptop bag and opens it.

"Look at that," he says, "a wide-screen Toshiba, looks like a late model, too. That will be expensive." The pawnshop owner's wife is standing next to them.

"If that's the one you like, it's yours, I will sort it out with my husband, don't you worry."

"Are you sure? Here is your money back," says Kamin. "No, no, keep it," she insists, "run along now."

"Thank you very, very much," stammers Kamin, close to tears of joy. They rush back to the bakery with their unexpected double reward.

The baker and his wife are busy cleaning up but stop to listen to what we two boys – (well, one boy and one robot) tell them.

"You deserve it," says the baker, and gives us our pay, thanks us again and sends us home. "See you tomorrow."

"Bye, thank you," we shout in unison, both too excited to repeat the first day's events at home.

But will it really become my new home?

CHAPTER SIX

As Kamin and I enter the living room, Mr Gushiken sees the leather laptop case immediately.

"Did you win the Lottery, Kamin?" he asks.

"Wait, wait, wait, everybody, let me go first," insists Mrs Gushiken. "Please, sit down and listen to this.

"I got to see Mr Suzuki, the very nice owner of the factory from which Ah-to escaped from this morning. I told him Ah-to's story and – much alarmed – he sent for the person in charge right away and asked him: 'How can that be?'

"That man had something to hide, because he said, '100 robots were produced, but I must have been careless stacking them, because one entire row fell and broke: some had to be scrapped.' "All Mr Suzuki told him was: 'Make sure to file an insurance claim.' Turning to me, he said: 'Accidents can happen.' That was it, but – getting to his feet – he added: 'As the inspector can account for all of the days production, no robot is missing.' With that he let me go! I did not have to pay for the robot. How nice is that?

Ah-to, now you can stay here – there is no debt to be paid.

"By the way, Ah-to, you cleaned the apartment so well, I thought I had entered the wrong apartment. You are worth every yen I may have to pay for you. From now on, you must call me by my given name, 'Keiko', yes, Ah-to?"

"Thank you, Mrs … mmm … sorry, eh, Keiko." They all smile about my discomfort.

"You can call me, 'Akio', please," Kamin's father adds.

"Yes, sir …" More amusement follows.

Kamin looks at his mother, slightly puzzled by some parts of her story. "Mum, that quality inspector, is he a lanky sort of a guy with thick eyeglasses on a too-long nose?"

"Yes, do you know him?" she asks.

"No, I don't," replies Kamin. *Strange, real strange.*

"Now, that we had to listen to mother first, how was your day, Kamin?" asks Akio.

Instead of replying, Kamin takes his smart phone from his pocket, to hand the Facebook pictures around.

"I can't believe that it actually happened," I say. "It all happened so fast. The main thing is we got him and no one got hurt."

"Quite right. Now, Kamin, what's with the leather laptop case?" Akio demands.

"Dad, the woman that nearly lost her bag, gave it to us ..." Then Kamin repeats in detail to his parents the story from the pawn shop.

"Let me see the laptop," says Akio, after Kamin has finished. The boy dutifully hands over the bag to his Father, who opens it. When he takes out the portable computer, he immediately whistles through his teeth.

"Hey," he says, "that is a wide-screen Toshiba, top of the range. Let me plug it in and boot it up, I want to see what operating programme is on it." Akio, Kamin, and I stay up late, checking the laptop out after Keiko has excused herself and gone to bed.

Akio and Kamin are so focused on the new laptop, that they do not notice my head tip onto its side. Although I cannot move my limbs or speak, I can still hear their conversation.

"Hey, Ah-to, what's up?" asks Kamin, "Did you fall asleep?"

"Robots don't sleep," says his father, "their batteries simply run

flat. You need to plug him into the mains circuit."

"Of course, you are right. Ah-to behaves like such a real person, I forget he is a robot," says Kamin.

"Wait until I start tweaking his software," says Akio, who, with his slicked back hair, and frameless glasses, looks every bit like a proper scientist. "He will become even more human than you."

"Can you do that?" asks Kamin in awe.

"I will have a look at what he has got inside him. After all, I am a software programmer. Perhaps I can supercharge him."

"Oh, man, just think what we could do," says Kamin.

"Off to bed now and don't forget to plug him in, the charger cord is there under his chest-plate. Do you see it?"

"Yes, I see it," replies Kamin. "Good night, Dad."

CHAPTER SEVEN

"Come over here, Ah-to," says Kamin's father on Sunday morning after breakfast. He is eager to have a look at my workings.

"Sorry," he says, "I have to switch you off, take out your hard drive, and copy the data to my laptop, to see how you are configured, what makes you tick, so to speak," says Akio.

"OK," I say, "I guess it's time for a snooze for me. See you later."

Kamin watches his father switch off the robot, before taking off the red breastplate. Inside is a solid-state battery, the hard drive, and what looks like millions of wires, connecting to all the different movement mechanisms.

"Look at that," says Mr Gushiken, "we are lucky that there is still so much space in there. I could fit a second battery, plus another hard drive with several Terabytes, instead of this small hard drive. Our Ah-to could become a walking encyclopaedia!" After copying the robot's existing programme to his laptop, he spends a couple of minutes more peering around inside.

"He is really well made," Akio marvels. "This is not a cheaply put-together toy."

Kamin is bent cosily beside his father, taking pictures with his smart phone of Otto's inner workings. After a while he says, "I didn't realise how much goes on inside a robot. He must be very expensive. I don't think Mom realised how much she might have had to pay for him."

"You are right, son," his father agrees. "We may not have been able to afford him."

"But here we are: it was all meant to be," says Kamin.

"Yes," says his father, "just like your laptop."

"Boy, oh boy, what a week we are having!" Kamin says, as Akio closes Otto up and prepares to switch him back on again.

"Any hope for me?" I ask after my re-boot.

"You are virtually hollow, look at you: wires and tiny motors – that's all there is to you," says Kamin, scrolling through the pictures with me.

"Let me see what I can find. Parts are getting cheaper, unless you are forced to buy brand names," says Akio.

Later that evening, Kamin and I are watching videos of the latest drone technology on the new laptop.

"Hey, that looks good," says Kamin, "I would love to build one of those from a kit box."

"You think you could?" I ask.

"Sure, I can start small and learn as I go," says Kamin, "I know a large store that sells all sorts of hobby stuff in kit-form. We are not working tomorrow, so why don't we have a look? We still have our reward money."

"I gave mine to your father, for parts for me," I say.

"Hey, I didn't know that. That's very smart of you," says Kamin. "It's what you might call investing in advanced education." I smile, tapping my chest, instead of my head.

"You know what?" says Kamin, putting an arm on my shoulder, "suddenly I have a brother that just popped up out of nowhere."

"Thank you," I say, bowing to him. "That's nice of you to say. I feel that too."

"If you could only wear my clothes," says Kamin, "people might actually think so."

"Not possible, I am afraid," I tell him, "but you could get a robot outfit, then we would have everybody fooled. Just imagine: two robots walking around together, talking like two intelligent humans." Then we both pack up laughing at the thought of it.

On the following Monday afternoon, I am waiting for Kamin

in the already clean apartment, when the doorbell rings. Before I can answer the door, I hear Kamin's voice in the stairwell, arguing with someone loudly. A moment later, he lets himself in with his swipe-card.

"These door-to-door salesmen are such a nuisance," he says. "Never answer the doorbell, no matter how long it chimes. We all have swipe-cards to get in. Once you start talking to those salesmen, you will never get rid of them."

"I see," I muse. "Do you think they would start a conversation with a robot?"

"Maybe not," replies Kamin shrugging his shoulders impatiently. "Come on, let's go."

The next unexpected incident occurs at the Metro station: Kamin swipes his season ticket and gets onto the escalator without thinking about me. I am stopped short by the turnstile. Realising his mistake, Kamin tries to race back up again. The crowd going down gets in his way, so he ends up by going all the way down and doubling back up again on the opposing escalator.

By this time, an impatient queue has formed around me, pushing, urging me on. I am standing helpless at the turnstile. Their increasing shouts of: "Move on! Hey, you, move on!" attract a Metro supervisor.

"Where is your ticket?" he demands. "You need to get a ticket over there at the ticket machine."

Somewhat confused, I look around. "It's him," I hear a young girl say. "It's him. I saw him on Facebook. He caught a bag-snatcher with his SpeCial's board."

An even larger crowd is now forming around me.

Kamin pushes his way through the gaping commuters: "Excuse me, please. Excuse me, he is with me."

A minute later, the supervisor opens a side-gate for us and waves us through. "Sorry Ah-to," says Kamin. "I forgot that you have never been on a Metro before. We will get you a season ticket for next time," says Kamin.

The Hobbies4us mega-store is huge, spread over four or five floors. Big boards, next to the escalators, give information of what is available on each floor. On the way up, I spot a section with costume displays: Superman, Spiderman, Terminator and – to my surprise – robot outfits just like my own.

"Look over there, Kamin!" I shout, pointing to them, "robot

outfits. Let's go see what they got on the way down."

Two floors higher up, we find the drones in a corner next to model helicopters. The drones range from miniatures to models with more than a metre span. Kamin finds, what he calls, a starter kit. "That will do for now. Let's go to the costume section," he says, pleased with his choice of drone.

Ten minutes later, the two of us have the whole robot outfit, identical to mine but with a blue trim for Kamin, instead of my red trim, Kamin pays for his purchases with just enough change to buy me a metro ticket.

On the way out of the mega-store, Kamin excuses himself to go to the public toilet and emerges a good ten minutes later, dressed as a robot, with his own clothes wrapped in the carrier-bag.

"Hey, now you look like me," I laugh.

On the Metro ride home, passengers stare at us. One old man mutters to his wife: "What are today's youth coming to? All comic- book characters. Nobody wants to be themselves anymore."

CHAPTER EIGHT

When Kamin and I burst into the apartment, Akio and Keiko get a big fright.

"Two robots? Where is Kamin? Ah-to, what is going on?!" they are just about shouting.

"It's me, Mother," says Kamin quickly pulling his helmet off. "Look, Ah-to has red trim; my trim is blue."

"Confusing, I must admit, "says Akio looking closely at them. "Where did you get the outfit?" asks Keiko, trying to calm down. To break the tension, the two relate the day's adventures, to his parents' great amusement.

"I hope you two don't cause trouble. The Tokyo police are very strict when it comes to misbehaving youth," Keiko admonishes.

"We promise," we reply together.

Later that evening, Akio says: "I checked with some colleagues of mine at work who conduct research on robotics. They think it will be possible to 'tweak', or improve you, Ah-to. One colleague knows something about the robots that are produced in the factory you come from. He says that they make many different models but that you are a basic domestic model, which can be upgraded at any stage – at a price of course – that's how they make their money. They get a basic robot like you into a household and once the robot has been accepted as part of their life, most owners will upgrade their companions. We will do it with our own parts, saving lots of money. Plus, I can programme you to a much higher level as we go."

This gets me to thinking, already. "I would like that," I say.

"Can you make me as smart as Kamin, then we will become known as the 'nerd twins'."

Kamin grabs me right away in a rugby tackle. "Who is a nerd? Who are you calling a nerd?" he squeals, pulling me with him onto the floor.

"Stop it! Stop it at once, you two!" Keiko demands trying to hide a smile because she has never seen Kamin so happy. "Really, this household used to be so peaceful and quiet. Now look what's happening. We are going to get complaints from the neighbours soon."

Disentangling ourselves, we promise to behave and go to our room to start with the assembly of the small, starter drone.

Before going to the bakery the next afternoon, Kamin makes a phone call. He disconnects after talking for less than a minute. "Check this out," he says to me, "we are going to have some fun this afternoon." He disappears into our bedroom and comes back out a moment later in his robot outfit. "Let's go. The bakery will never be the same again." Little does he know how true his words will prove to be.

When we get there, the arcade is still quiet; the rush hour has not started yet. Closer to the bakery, however, they see more and more teenagers hanging out.

"Hey, look at that! There are two robots today!" shouts one young girl.

"I don't believe it! Look at that!" screams another.

Kamin and I have a problem getting through.

"There are two robots! Look!"

Mr and Mrs Yamashita both have huge smiles in their already round faces when the two robots push their way into the shop. The baker has a big tray in front of him with icing bags on the worktop. He is putting the finishing touches to a tray of robot-shaped biscuits.

"This is his third tray," says his wife, wiping pearls of perspiration of her nose: "They are selling like hotcakes." Realising her word play, she giggles, pushing another robot biscuit into another outstretched hand that is waving money at her.

She barely has time to ask: "Who is who here now?"

"Ah-to has the red trim, mine is blue," says Kamin.

"Well, then," says the baker, we will just call you 'Red' and 'Blue' in future, instead of Ah-to and Kamin, that's much easier, but come, you two, help me with the next two trays. Who wants to do the white icing and who wants to do the red or blue piping?" "We'll take turns," we reply. "That way we can learn both jobs." With rush-hour in full swing the four of us are working flat out. The baker is mixing dough, rolling it out, cutting the robot shapes, baking them, and placing the hot biscuits on cooling racks – he never stops.

The two robots are mixing white icing; dividing batches to add red or blue food colouring; remixing; spreading white icing; piping the colours; handing the finished trays to Mrs Yamashita, who bags them, hands them over the counter, and stuffs the money into her apron pocket, having no time to open and close the cash register. The far-too small bakery is a madhouse.

"No need for the SpeCial's board today: it's only robot biscuits, red or blue," she laughs.

By 9.30 p.m. the baker tells the few waiting customers: "That's the last tray for tonight, more tomorrow."

"Can you make take-away boxes with six and twelve biscuits, please. We want to take them home for our families," asks one teenager, as she collects the last robot biscuit.

"Now look what you two have done," says the baker, wiping his smiling, sweating face with the upturned corners of his apron, "I will be here all night."

"We can stay on and help," I offer.

"Easy for you Mr Robot, you don't need sleep, just a new battery pack," says Kamin, more as a joke than a complaint, before phoning his parents for permission to work until midnight. "Here you are Red/Blue: double pay for both of you. Thank you so much," says the tired baker at midnight. Looking at the clock, he adds "see you this afternoon."

Although Kamin is dead tired, they still skip and trot all the way home, happy with the extra money.

On the following Thursday afternoon, Kamin's smart phone interrupts his homework.

"Hello, Mr Yamashita," says Kamin and switches the phone to "speaker" for me to hear.

"Listen, you two," says the baker, "can you get another robot outfit, same size as yours?" asks the baker.

"Who for? For Mrs Yamashita by any chance?" asks Kamin.

"Don't get smart with me," says the baker, "no, it's not for my wife. I have an idea – just get another outfit, maybe with green or black piping."

"We can do that," says Kamin, "we may be a couple of minutes late for our shift."

"No problem. See you later." The phone bleeps to say that he has hung up.

This time our trip to the hobby mega-store, is without incident, other than all the comments we attract on the Metro, especially from older commuters.

In the store they buy an identical outfit with black armbands and rush back to the bakery.

Mr Yamashita has a child mannequin, a window dresser's model, behind the counter. He quickly dresses the plastic figure and stands it in the shops window, with a six-pack box of robot biscuits secure in its hands.

"Doesn't hurt to advertise," he says, repaying Kamin's expenses. It will be a week or ten days, before the bakery returns to its full menu of specials again, and I am able to resume carrying the A-frame up and down the arcade. But by this time I am well known and everyone greets me by name, often asking: "Hey Ah-to, caught any more bag snatchers?"

My smiling reply is always the same: "No snatchers in this arcade while I'm on duty!"

CHAPTER NINE

On the following Sunday morning, Mr Gushiken asks Kamin and me to stay in the apartment. He has cleared the dining-room table, covered it with a soft tablecloth, and laid out several small, labelled boxes.

Kamin and I pull up chairs to watch Akio's preparations as he lays out small tools neatly in front of him. His own laptop is switched on, with a USB cable attached to one of its ports. "Ah-to, it's sleep time for you, hopefully for the last time," he says.

"Just when it gets interesting, I get switched off," I groan in mock protest.

"Don't worry," says Kamin, "I will video everything father does to you."

Akio switches the robot off and opens the breastplate to remove the existing solid-state battery. From one of the boxes he carefully unpacks a tandem battery pack: two batteries mounted on a bracket next to each other. In between the two batteries is a small electronic switch.

"I have fitted two solid-state batteries to this bracket," he explains to Kamin. "When one runs low, it will activate an alarm, to inform Ah-to of his low-battery status. This switch will automatically change over to the second battery, to keep Ah-to active. Now he has 24 hours to plug himself in for a re-charge."

Kamin asks: "Does that mean, with both batteries fully charged, Ah-to can keep going for 48 hours?"

"Even longer," says his father, "depending on how active he is. When he has saved up more money, I can buy another twin-pack that you could exchange for him to keep him going forever."

"I wish I could go without rest or sleep for weeks on end," says Kamin, "I could do twice as much each day, instead of wasting time sleeping."

Akio nods: "That's why a lot of factories now have automated assembly lines. They never have to stop, other than for maintenance.

"Right," Akio continues, "the battery pack is sorted out. Now we tackle the hard drive. The prices are coming down fast. One Terabyte costs less now than one Gigabyte a year ago. Plus: they are getting smaller and smaller. Look in here." He points at Otto's open chest cavity. "There is his battery, and there, further down the spine is the hard drive."

Kamin moves closer with his smart phone to record Otto's interior construction. "Why is the hard drive mounted so low in his body?" he asks his father.

"To keep him balanced. They kept the heavier parts lower down in his body," says Akio. "This new hard drive I am going to put in is quite a bit heavier, because of the increased capacity of ten Terabytes."

"Ten Terabyte? What on earth can we store on there?" asks Kamin.

"Wait until I have it all connected; then we can switch Ah-to back on and connect him to my laptop to work on his software," says Akio with a big smile. "I have a couple of ideas up my sleeve."

"Please, tell me, I can't wait," begs his son.

"One thing at a time; be patient," says his father, pulling more bits and pieces out of packets.

"Come and have your lunch," orders Keiko from the kitchen counter.

"Mo-om, do we have to? Can't you keep it for us? We are really busy right now," whines Kamin. He has been holding a spotlight over Otto's open chest armour, to provide lots of light for his father to work inside the cavity.

Mrs Gushiken relents. "I'll leave it on the counter to help yourselves. I am having something now because I am hungry." She smiles to herself, happy to see her husband and son so deeply immersed together in their joint project.

"OK," says Akio, half an hour later, locking the breastplate in position, "let's wake your brother up."

Even though Otto is switched back on, nothing happens.

"Father – what have you done? Is he dead? He's not opening his eyes! His head is all lopsided! His arms and legs are just stretched out. What is wrong with him?!" Kamin is close to tears.

Akio smiles: "Don't worry, my son. I took out his small hard drive that controls his mechanism. Look: it's right here, connected to my laptop. All I need to do is transfer the data from this old drive to the new one I have just installed. All should be working again."

"Should? Are you sure?" asks Kamin, wiping his face with his hands nervously.

"Quite sure," says his father in his most reassuring tone, hoping deep down that he is right. For the next ten or fifteen minutes, which seem like hours to an anxious Kamin, Akio concentrates on transferring data from the old to the new hard drive via his laptop.

Slowly I open my eyes, look around, bewildered, and ask: "W-w-where am I?" I stutter incoherently.

"Stay still for a bit longer," says Akio, "the data is still transferring, movement by movement."

Over the next few minutes, I feel myself returning to my old self again, as if (I have heard them say) recovering from an anaesthetic after surgery in a hospital.

"What a weird feeling!" I say, testing all my movements, "parts of me refuse to function."

Keiko, who has come over to join them, shares the greatly relieved sighs of her son.

CHAPTER TEN

Kamin and I have no problems assembling the small, beginner's drone. Having explicit instructions in its box, as well as internet links to videos which explain the assembly step-by-step, we proceed faster than we had hoped for.

On the following Monday afternoon, Kamin gets used to the remote-control transmitter for the drone. He is sitting on his laptop with a drone-simulator programme coupled to his hand-held, remote control, practising take-off and landing, and right and left turns.

"Come on, come on!" I urge him, jumping in front of him. "That's enough with the simulation. Let's fly it from here: nothing can happen."

I know I am right. The beginner model is small enough to fly in our bedroom, using the futon for a soft, safe landing field.

Kamin and I have agreed to share all belongings, simply calling them "our stuff". We see no need for "mine" or "yours" from now on. On this afternoon, we take turns with the drone and on the simulator, keeping ourselves equally amused.

Akio has shown me how I can add data to my new hard drive by connecting myself to the laptop via the USB port. "So much to learn," we both groan, for different reasons.

I find a bigger drone simulator app on the laptop, teaching me how to fly more advanced drone models. "Kamin, look at this," I call out. "This drone can lift 30 kg and deliver that load to a customer faster than by car."

Kamin lands his little drone expertly on the table next to the laptop in order to focus on the video.

"Wow! Look at that!" he exclaims. "I wonder how much one of

these drones will cost?"

I click on the drone manufacturer's website; select the model I have been watching in action.

"Rotor span: 3,2 metres," I read out aloud. "Maximum payload: 30 kg. Maximum operating time: 30 minutes. Price: US $11,500 plus shipping. Radio transmitter excluded."

"What?!" Kamin cries out, completely shocked, "That's nearly *1.3 MILLION* yen, we will never be able to afford one of those."

"What on earth for?" I ask him, surprised by my brother's outburst. "Haven't you seen the videos of all the things they are using drones for: surveillance, aerial photography, security work and, deliveries. They deliver medicine, blood for emergency transfusion, even supermarket groceries."

"Really?" says Kamin. "We could do deliveries for the bakery," he adds jokingly.

"Hey, that's a brilliant idea!" I tell Kamin, getting serious. "Takeaway lunches, why not? But then: where are we going to get the money for such a big drone from? It will never happen."

"I suppose you are right," shrugs Kamin. Then, looking at his clock he says: "Shall we go to Hobbies4us and see what other models they have got in our price range?"

"Sure, let's go," I reply. "Looking doesn't cost anything. By the way, what is our price range?"

"I don't know," he says, on his way to change into his robot outfit, before hastily scribbling a note to let his parents know where we have gone.

"There they are, there they are!" shouts a young Hobbies4us sales assistant to one of his colleagues, as Kamin and I come up on the escalator. "Excuse me guys," he says, stopping us as we reach his floor.

"Something wrong?" asks Kamin, alarmed by the man's behaviour.

"No, no – sorry," says the assistant, apologetically. "I didn't mean to startle you. It's just that our sales manager asked us to look out for you. He wants a word with you. Please, would you mind coming with me to his office?"

"What's it all about?" I ask him.

"No idea," says the assistant, rushing us down a narrow passage with offices on either side, before stopping in front of a closed door marked: "ₛₐₗₑₛ ₍dₑₚₐRₜMₑNₜ₎". Then we hear a voice from inside calling: "Come in!" and the assistant opens the door. Behind a massive desk, overflowing with boxes and papers, sits a stout man, in his late forties, shirt sleeves rolled up to his elbows, and thin-rimmed spectacles pushed high up on his forehead. The brass plate on his desk displays his name as: "Takahashi, Daiki; Hobbies4us; Sales Manager".

"The two boys you wanted to have a word with are here, Mr Takahashi," says the sales assistant, bowing respectfully to his manager.

"Oh, yes," he beams. "Come in, come right in, please," dismissing our escort with a wave of his pudgy hand. "Who is who with you two?" he asks, looking from one to the other.

"Does it matter?" asks Kamin.

"No, not really," replies the manager "just nice to know." "Red for robot, blue for boy. Easy to remember," I say.

"Ah, alright," says Mr Takahashi. Not one who likes to waste time, he comes straight to the point.

"Here is my plan for you two, Red and Blue. As you surely know, you have become quite famous on Twitter and Facebook since you brought down that bag snatcher. Then again in the bakery: with queues running down the main road, for the Robot biscuits. Very good, by the way, my daughter brought a six-pack home, of which I ate four," he says, licking his lips.

"To the point," he continues. "We sold out all our robot costumes within days. I am getting a new shipment in later in the week. I want to hire you to be on our floor. To do promotions for your outfits; but also, for other things, such as table-tennis, skateboarding, roller-blades – you know: that sort of thing." He breaks off, rubbing his hands together, waiting for our reaction.

"How much?" I ask.

"Why, I would have thought that robots don't have any use for money," cackles Mr Takahashi, feigning surprise.

"Oh, but I do," I say quickly. "I fly drones now. Do you know how expensive they are? They are eating up all my money ... and his," I say, pointing at the nodding Kamin.

"Very expensive," Kamin chimes in. "We are talking millions of yen here. How are we going to get so much money, if we work for free?"

"I see. I see. You have picked an expensive hobby indeed. Here is what I can do for you. I will sign you up as part-time promotions staff. That way I can pay you a fee, commission, while you will also qualify for our 50 percent staff discount. Yes, 50 percent: you heard right. Mark up on hobby goods is high, but we give our employees the benefits so that they can afford to buy some of the items, things, to show them to their friends, so that they come and buy them, too. It's called 'peer pressure', you understand that, don't you?"

"Yes, we know all about that," says Kamin, nodding in agreement. "The problem is that we work in the bakery, Wednesdays to Fridays. We could only work on Saturdays."

"Can you work Saturday and Sunday? Those are our busiest days," says Mr Takahashi.

Kamin looks at me: "What do you think?"

"I'm OK, I am a robot, as long as my batteries are charged, I am good to go. What about you though? Your homework?" I say. "Let's give it a go, we will always have Mondays and Tuesdays. Besides, with you next to me, my homework goes much faster, less distractions," says Kamin.

"Can I take that as a 'yes'?" asks Takahashi, Daiki.

"Yes, Mr Takahashi, we will give it a try," I say, bowing politely. And thank you for offering us the staff discount. We really appreciate it. Now to the salary and commission. What do you have in mind?"

Takahashi rubs his hands once more, looks up to the ceiling, and purses his lips, before replying.

"I will pay you 2,000 yen per day," he says, "basic, plus a five percent commission on the promotion you are doing for us that day."

"Sir," I ask, "did you not say that the mark-up on hobby goods is high?"

"Yes, that is so …"

"Can you then not make the commission ten percent? It is easier for us kids to calculate."

Takahashi bursts out laughing. "I like your reasoning, Red," he says. "OK then, ten percent it is. Now that we are all agreed, you can call me Daiki. All the staff call me by my given name. I will see you on Saturday. Be here before 9 a.m., if you can."

"Sure thing, Daiki," we reply as one.

Out of earshot, back in the store, Kamin high-fives me.

"I like your style, brother: *'Ten percent is easier to calculate for us kids.'* Let's go home, it's getting late. Now that we are members of staff, we will have lots of opportunity to look at drones and get some advice from our new colleagues."

Akio and Keiko are stunned by our story: the job offer, the salary, the commission and the staff-discount. Akio looks at me with a proud smile in his face and says: "My tweak has turned you into a smart negotiator. Maybe I should be entitled to a share of your commission. I can see the good influence you have on our son as well."

"We are a team," I reply. "More than a team: we are brothers. Thanks to you, Keiko, for going to the factory with the intention of buying me. I have to thank Kamin for inviting me in the first place, and then all of you for taking me into your home, accepting me as part of your family."

"Stop. Stop it," whispers Keiko, "you are making me all tearful.

Get your dinner, you two – oh, sorry, I forgot you are a robot."

On the next Wednesday afternoon, Kamin and I are back at the bakery and the Yamashita's are all smiles.

"Business has never been so good," says Mrs Yamashita. "We need to employ a second baker. My poor husband is working far too late into the night."

"Ah-to, do you think I could teach you?" asks Mr Yamashita.

"You most probably could, but I don't want to become a baker

with no future." Mr Yamashita looks hurt, because he did not expect that reply.

Kamin, jumps in: "No, don't misunderstand Ah-to, what he says is true. Machines are replacing people ..."

"I know that," says the baker, still not happy, "but the goods made by machine don't taste the same, do they? That's why people come to us."

Kamin can see the baker's irritation and changes tactics. "Mr Yamashita, what do you spend most of your time on: preparing or baking?"

Without hesitation the baker replies: "The preparation, of

course, the baking does not take up my personal time, only the oven. It's the mixing, rolling, shaping, icing and decorating that takes the time."

Kamin says: "Don't we know it from the robot biscuits. Now, Mr Yamashita, may I just tell you something? Ah-to and I have been researching the latest technologies on the Internet, mainly to do with robotics, as you will understand. One interesting process we noticed is 3-D-printing. It is used to manufacture small volumes of complicated parts for machinery, for instance. But also to make food. We did not spend a lot of time on that particular application, but it looks interesting."

"Printing food?" says the baker, "What next? I wish I knew more about all this stuff. I'm behind the times with all this new technology.

"Say, you young ones are always on your PCs and smart phones: won't you look into it for me and see what you can find?" "Yes, boys," says Mrs Yamashita, "will you? We will pay you for your time."

I nod to Kamin, "We can do that, I have time on my hands when Kamin is at school or is busy with his homework. Leave it with us. Maybe Mr Gushiken knows something about it, too."

CHAPTER ELEVEN

Just before 8.45 a.m. on the following Saturday morning, we are knocking on the door of Daiki's office.

"Come in!" we hear him shout. He is perched behind his huge desk, which is laden with sample boxes and paperwork.

"There you are Red and Blue," he cackles cheer-fully. "Right on time, I like that. OK, let's not waste time; I took a chance on you two and got in 100 robot outfits. This is what I propose: Robot costume promotion: price: 50,000 yen; commission 5,000 yen each." He hands Kamin the piece of paper with his calculations. Kamin's mind is trying to grasp the numbers, but I am faster.

"Times 100; that is 500,000 yen, plus our salary of 4,000 yen for the day, right?"

"Quite right, if you hit the target, you could be half millionaires by tomorrow night."

"Why tomorrow? How about tonight?" asks Kamin, quite dizzy from trying to grasp the numbers.

"Dream on," says Daiki with a huge smile. "We have NEVER sold more than ten or twelve outfits per weekend. The only reason I bought 100 sets is the high quantity discount the manufacturer gave me. If we sell them over the next three to four months, I am happy. Have you thought about what you will do to promote sales?"

"Well, yes, of course ..." says Kamin, but the truth is that we have not thought about it at all, thinking that Daiki, as a sales manager, would tell us what to do.

"Good, well, that's it, boys. Don't let me stop you from becoming full millionaires," he cackles once again while returning to his paperwork.

"So? What's your plan?" I ask in the passage to the store.

"My plan?" Kamin exclaims. "I thought you were the brains of this team. Haven't you worked out a plan yet?"

"No, not a clue," I reply. "Let's just go to the outfit section and take it from there, shall we?" We make our way through the store to the escalator that will take us up to the outfit floor.

"Look! There are those two robots," I hear from behind us. I turn to see two young girls, pointing and giggling.

"Hello, good morning," I say in a high female voice, "I wish we were those two, but, at least with these outfits on, we can look like them," I add with a girlish giggle.

"You are a girl? We thought all robots are guys," says the braver one of the two.

"Not so," I giggle. "This is the best way to fool guys though, don't you think?"

"It's so cool," says the brave girl, looking at her friend. "What do you think, shall we try it on?"

"The outfits are over there, let's go," I shrill. "Come I'll show you."

I take the teenager by the hand and literally run with her through the aisles, attracting lots of attention.

"I only hope they are not sold out again, my friend got the last one on Wednesday," I shriek excitedly.

Two teenage boys nudge each other and follow us.

"Look there they are," I say, pointing at the shelf advertising the promotion. "What colour do you want?"

Then I pretend to be surprised, "I don't believe it!" I shriek, my voice even higher, "a promotion, we paid nearly double. It's your lucky day!"

The two boys push us aside, "Excuse us, *LADIES*, while you make up your minds, let us take what we want."

"You see, I told you, they'd sell quickly. You are so lucky to get the promotion on top of it."

"Thank you so much," say the two girls, clutching their outfits protectively to themselves.

"Mummy, can I have one, *PLEASE*," begs a little boy, maybe eight or nine years old.

"Let me pick you up," says Kamin, advancing toward the mother and her son. "You are lucky, I paid nearly double. You want red, green, blue or black?"

"Take the violet one up there," says the mother. "It's the only one in that colour. "With Kamin holding him he takes the violet suit off the shelf. "Better take the yellow one for your brother, otherwise the two of you will fight non-stop."

The boy takes the two outfits, wiggles away from Kamin: "Thank you for lifting me up," he says, hanging on to his outfits.

"That worked OK," says Kamin when they are alone again, "six outfits in less than half an hour. By the way, I like your squeaky voice."

"A promotor has to be versatile," I laugh.

"Excuse me, can I take a picture of us," says another teenage girl, with a smart phone on a selfie stick.

"Sure you can," I say in my female voice again.

"You are a girl?" she asks surprised.

"No, I am a robot. We can be anything we want to be," I say, this time in my normal voice.

"Why don't you put on one of these outfits, too, and then we take the selfie," suggests Kamin in a female voice this time.

"You guys are funny. Yes, give me an outfit, I'll put it on in the change room after I have paid. Please pass me one with orange trim," she says.

A moment later, she is back; having changed into her robot outfit, her street clothes in a shopping bag. More shoppers stop and stare, as the three of us pose for the selfies. Kamin and I lift the girl onto our shoulders to loud applause and squeals of laughter.

The crowd around us is growing, as more youngsters are picking outfits for themselves.

"Wait for us, we'll go and change, then we can make a pyramid," suggest two boys.

"Good idea," I say, urging them to hurry. "Let's wait for them." "We should move to the end of the aisle where we have more space," suggests Kamin, picking up the promotion sign to take with. Fifteen minutes later, the pyramid that had started out with five robots, has grown to seven, then to nine.

Kamin and I have extracted ourselves from the growing pyramid, passing outfits to a queue of eager buyers. The ever-growing crowd is cheering. Other floor salesmen have come to steady the pyramid.

Mr Takahashi is standing right next to the pyramid, insisting on being in all the pictures. He knows that they will be all over

Facebook and Twitter in minutes.

Kamin and I bring trolley after trolley, filled with robot outfits, place them next to the promotion sign. The pyramid grows; changes, the base gets wider as they attempt to go higher.

The laughter and shouts of encouragement from the spectators draws more and more attention to the robots – and the promotion. More outfits are brought from the storeroom, soon to be sold.

At closing time, Daiki calls them into his office. He is sitting in front of his computer, looking at the sales figures for the day:

"Look at this, just look at this! Forty-two robot outfits sold in one day! I can't believe that I was so naïve to let you talk me into paying you a ten percent commission."

"Don't worry Daiki," says Kamin," the money will come straight back to you."

"How so?" the sales manager asks.

"We are saving up for a bigger drone," says Kamin, "and they are very expensive."

Daiki looks at them with new interest. "You guys any good with drones?"

"Not yet," I say. "We only have a beginner's kit so far, and we don't yet have the money for another, bigger model."

Daiki gets up, goes to a shelving unit covering one wall and shifts some boxes around in search of something. He then hauls a fair-sized box off a lower shelf and says: "This is a sample that a new supplier dropped off. Wants me to stock it. I need to test it, to form an opinion. No good sitting there in its box, is it? Can you two put it together, test it for me; maybe demonstrate it in the shop, as part of your promotion: 'Robots Fly Drones' – that would look good on Twitter, wouldn't it?"

Kamin has jumped up as Daiki spells it out for us. "Sure, we would love to do that for you," he says.

"I am sure you would," Daiki smirks. "Have a go. Maybe we

can run a promotion next weekend."

"Gee, thank you, Daiki," we both say, leaving his office with the drone-kit box carefully carried between us.

On the Metro home, Kamin says to me: "Not a bad start for the first day, is it? Nearly quarter of a million yen earned, with a drone to assemble thrown in."

"Quite so, young man," I reply with my girly voice, to add in my normal voice, "we need to make a list of the projects we are working on; and make a time-table, so that we don't let anything slip, like your homework, for example."

"You are beginning to sound like my father," Kamin complains. "Has he by any chance tweaked his brain into you?"

"Maybe he has, who knows?" I laugh, "I just don't want you to get into trouble, or to let anybody down,"

"You are right, thank you," says Kamin.

Akio and Keiko are sitting in the living room when the two of us walk in with the big drone-kit box. "What is that?" asks Akio.

"It's a new drone model that has been offered to Mr Takahashi, Daiki, the sales manager at Hobbies4us. Before he adds it to his range of stock, he wants us to test it. He asked us tonight if we could do that for him."

Akio scratches his head in amazement. "You two sure know how to wangle things your way: free laptop, free drone testing, weekend promotions! Talking of which: how did it go today? Did you manage to sell a couple of robot outfits?"

Instead of answering his father, Kamin pulls out his smart phone and shows them the Facebook page with the pyramid pictures,

"Look at that!" gasps Keiko. "I don't believe what I am seeing. Look at all the likes and comments … thousands of them."

Akio looks at the two boys with new respect: "How on earth did you manage that?"

"It started by my pretending to be a girl-robot," I say in my squeaky voice.

Keiko shrieks with laughter: "I don't believe this. Look at all these kids in robot outfits. You say girls bought them as well?"

"They sure did, when they thought Ah-to was a female robot. 'Cool', is what they said."

Akio wipes tears of merriment from his eyes, to ask: "So, how many outfits did you sell?"

I smile in return. "About forty, we guess, according to Daiki."

"He must be really pleased with you two," says Akio. "Now I

understand why he gave you the drone to assemble: as a special 'Thank you bonus', I think."

"I don't know," I tell him. "He was squealing about the 10% commission he agreed to pay us."

It does not take long for Kamin to go to sleep, after plugging me in for my recharge. It has been a long, action-filled day, even for me, a mere robot.

In the morning, long before 9 a.m., curious passers-by watch the queue of teenagers waiting for Hobbies4us to open its doors.

"What is going on?" enquires an elderly man from one of the waiting teenagers. "The two robots are here for a promotion," replies the youth.

Shaking his head, the elderly man pushes his way through the queue. "Excuse me," he says, "may I get through?"

Kamin does not notice the same lanky man that had spoken to him in the arcade. He barely has time to remove the last trolley full of robot outfits from the store, when the pushing and shoving teenage crowd, intermingled with anxious parents, get up to their floor on the escalator.

Some impatient kids even race up the stairs. According to the respectful Japanese tradition, however, the kids automatically form a queue in front of the promotions board.

Kamin and I are surprised to see another, taller robot in a much too tight outfit, stand next to another trolley, shooting a video of the promotion.

"Who are you?" I ask. The taller robot lifts his helmet, to reveal a sweating Takahashi, Daiki with a huge grin in his face:

"We are going to sell out before lunch, by the looks of things!" he shouts, jumping up and down, while pushing his helmet back into place.

Not quite, because it is closer to three o'clock when we knock on the sales manager's door.

"Come in!" they hear him shout again. As usual he is perched behind his mess of a desk.

"We have sold out," Kamin announces, his helmet under his

arm, wiping his damp hair out of his face. "What can we do until closing time? We have no more outfits to promote."

"Go home. You can start assembling the drone," he says. "Go home and get to it. Phone me if you feel you are ready to demonstrate it by next Saturday, OK? Oh, Kamin, one more thing; have you got a bank account?"

"No Mr … eh sorry, Daiki, I have not," says Kamin.

"Open one, and text me the details, that I can arrange for a transfer of your first weekend's earnings."

We can't get out fast enough: Over half a million yen in under two days, plus a big drone to assemble.

CHAPTER TWELVE

"You are home early," Keiko greets us.

"You are not going to believe this," says Kamin. "*We sold out!* Daiki told us to go home early and start work on the big drone. Say, Mum, can I get my own bank account?" asks Kamin, still breathless from racing me up the stairs to our apartment.

"Yes, you can," his mother replies. "As a minor it would be best for you to do it at the Post Bank. All you need is your ID document; you don't even need us."

"Great," Kamin says. "We will do it tomorrow. Daiki needs the account details for his office to transfer our commission and salary."

When we are seated once more in our room, Kamin wants to open the big drone's box immediately, but I stop him.

"Wait a moment," I say. "Let's first write up a day-by-day planner for both of us first, so that we keep our priorities in order." "Here we go again," Kamin groans. "Alright then, if you insist." "Have you learned how to create a spreadsheet in your computer classes?" I ask him.

"Yes, I have, but it's some time ago, and, frankly, as we have never used it, I forgot. When we are in the computer room at school, the lecturer gives us projects, or videos to watch, while he sits and answers his e-mails, or responds to his social media messages. So, we do the same – behind his back, of course."

"I see. Well, you better pay attention now." Then I open a blank spreadsheet and start to explain.

"We create eight vertical columns," I say, one for each day of the week, plus one extra. Next, we go to this far left column –

the first one – and create horizontal rows with times of the day. Your school starts at eight, so you write '8.00' in the first box, underneath '9.00', then '10.00' all the way through to '22.00' or 10 p.m., when we are supposed to go to sleep. Got it?"

"Oh, yes," says Kamin, "I remember now. In each square of, say, the Monday column, I can now enter what I need to be doing, right?"

"Yes, you got it. While you do that, I'll open the box and have a look what's inside."

"*NO! WAIT FOR ME!*" Kamin whines. "If you rummage in that box, I will not be able to concentrate on this spreadsheet."

"All right," I chide, "hurry up then!"

Over the following half-an-hour, I help him finish his day-by- day planner.

"How come you know all this stuff?" he asks, when we are done.

"I just know. It must have something to do with your father's new database installation. I just think about something and it comes to mind, instantly."

"That's amazing!" Kamin exclaims. "I wish I could do that …" "But you can," I interrupt him, "just open your laptop and ask the right question, and you get the answer. The only difference between you and me is that my browser is a built-in, thought- activated type. One day that technology will be available to all humans as well. It's called 'AHI' – or 'Advanced Human Intelligence' instead of 'AI' – or 'Artificial Intelligence'."

Kamin nods, trying to understand what I am suggesting.

Carefully, we open the drone's box to examine its content. Right on top is an envelope which contains the warranty papers and two DVDs. One DVD is labelled 'Assembly Instructions', on the sleeve, while the other reads 'Simulator'.

"Let's watch the Assembly DVD on the laptop first," Kamin pleads. "Then we can get an idea as to what we are in for."

At this moment Akio steps inside the door. Looking at the opened box, with the DVD in Kamin's hand, he says: "I am curious to see this, can I join you?"

"Of course," says his son. "We would love you to join us. We may need your help."

After Kamin places the DVD in the laptop, his father says: "I have an idea. Let's connect Ah-to via a USB to the laptop, then we can copy the content of the DVD to his hard drive. That way he will be able to follow the assembly, step by step, by replaying it in his mind."

Kamin and I look at him: "Do you think it will work?" I ask.

"It must work. You are a computer with a built-in ability to call up and replay any programme installed on your hard drive. Remember, I wrote the programme, for you to be able to do that, as part of your deep-learning function."

"That's awesome!" I respond. "Let's do it."

The DVD is transferred to my hard drive and we playback the assembly instructions by watching the laptop's widescreen.

"That's fantastic!" says Akio at the finish. "Just follow it step by step, you can't really go wrong now." Taking another look at the second enclosed DVD, he loads the simulator and flight-training programme as well. He then calls it up on the laptop browser and connects the games controller.

Five minutes later, Keiko rushes into the room to check what the noise and shouting is all about. She finds her three boys on the floor, twisting and turning, in tune with the drone flown by the simulator.

Akio jumps up, blushing just a little for being caught out by his wife, acting just like a teenage boy. It's ten o'clock already and the arrival of bedtime catches us by surprise. Where did the time go?

Day 1, Monday, according to their written programme, proceeds as planned. Kamin goes to school, while I clean the apartment. With time on my hands, I search for information on the 3-D-printing of cakes and confectionary; I watch about half-a-dozen videos before sharing the best links to Kamin's smart phone, via e-mail, so that he can show them to Mr Yamashita on Wednesday afternoon.

Having returned home later on, Kamin finishes his homework with me looking over his shoulder.

"Let's go to the Post Office," he urges, "to open a savings account for me." Kamin is eager to see their first Hobbies4you pay-cheque in his new account.

At the Post Office we are assisted by an extremely efficient female clerk to whom Kamin explains his requirements.

"These are your account details," she declares after a little while. "Send them to the sales manager that he can transfer your money. Have you got 1000 yen now to open your account?"

Kamin nods in agreement and pulls the money out of his pocket, before handing it over to the clerk.

"You can check your balance online," she says, "by downloading our App. Like this." She shows him how to do it on his smart phone.

"Thank you. That's great," he says.

Back home again, we lay out the drone kit as per the step-by-step video instruction: the platform, the frame, the rotors, the electric motors, the battery pack, the GPS, and the tiny camera.

Soon we are immersed in the assembly, only to be disturbed by Keiko's calls to come and eat. While Kamin is gulping down his *ramen,* a spicy chicken noodle soup, I tell our parents about the Post Office savings account.

"That is wonderful!" says Akio. "It's an easy way to learn how to grow your money."

"Hey, I nearly forgot, I need to send the account details to Daiki," says Kamin, reaching for his smart phone. That done, we excuse ourselves from the table to continue with the drone assembly until bedtime.

The drone kit came with all the small tools required to fit the multitude of parts together. Some pieces clip together; others need to be tightened with small screwdrivers and key-wrenches, or tiny spanners.

All is explained step by step as I can now replay the instruction video in my mind and know it off by heart. Now I guide Kamin as we go.

Slowly but surely we are finished late on Tuesday night. Akio comes into our room when he hears the six tiny electric motors start up and idle, ready for take-off.

"Don't worry," Kamin reassures his father quickly. "It's too big to lift off in here. We'll try it tomorrow in the courtyard."

"Well done, boys. That looks amazing. Now tell me: where are you going to sleep tonight? There is no room left, but – apart from that minor inconvenience –" he grins, "maybe you can give me a chance to fly it before you take it away to Hobbies4us on Saturday. By the way, how are you going to get it to the shop, anyway? Even with folded rotors the drone is too big for the Metro."

Kamin scratches his head, "We could hire a premium Uber taxi, like a Minivan, that should do it. I am sure Takahashi Daiki will pay for it."

"Better phone him tomorrow; he may have a better solution,"

says Akio, "Good night, I bet you'll sleep well tonight, with one leg over the body and the other over the rotors. Come Ah-to, you can stand in the passage, there is a plug for you," he says, taking me by the hand.

Back on duty at the bakery on Wednesday afternoon, Mr & Mrs Yamashita watch the 3-D-printing video several times, whenever they have a spare moment.

"You youngsters are right, I could never do what this 3-D-printer is doing," admits the baker, fascinated by this new technology. "I will definitely look into it, get some idea of prices. Maybe visit the supplier if it's not too far from here. Thank you for the research." On Thursday, the baker is not in the shop and his wife is running around, trying to cope on her own. I see what's going on and, with my increased photographic memory, automatically assume the role of the baker, mixing batches of dough, pre-heating the ovens, baking, and decorating.

Kamin and Mrs Yamashita are bombarded with orders as more and more customers flock into watch me, a robot, baking.

"He can bake, too," says one customer, "not just catch bag snatchers."

"He is a good investment for the baker," comments another. An elderly man with long, white hair is standing to one side of the counter, not looking at the food, but watching me and Kamin intently. We have never seen this customer in the bakery before.

Kamin approaches him. "May I help you, sir?" he asks, bowing respectfully.

"I can see that you are not a robot, just wearing the outfit. My name is Suzuki Shushumi. You can think of me as a kind of father," he says, pointing at Otto.

"What did you say, sir?" Kamin asks, not sure he had heard correctly.

The white-haired man smiles proudly: "I designed him, and all the other robot models we make in my factory just up the road."

Sensing that someone is talking about me, I turn away from my worktables and ovens to face the counter.

Kamin calls me over: "Ah-to, this is Mr Suzuki Shushumi – your father. What he means is that he designed your type of model."

Before I can say anything Mr Suzuki Shushumi says softly: "I know who the two of you are," turning slightly to include Kamin in the conversation, before continuing. "Your mother, Mrs Gushiken, came to pay for a robot that, she said, had escaped from our factory, when, in fact, we were not missing a robot."

The old man smiles and winks before continuing again. "I have been following the two of you on Facebook and Twitter; you have become quite the celebrities, with thousands of fans. I had to come and see you in person, so to speak, to find out your secret." "You have changed," he says to me. "You are not the robot I designed. Are you prepared to share your secret with me, your 'father'?" he asks in a whisper, extracting a business card from his breast pocket and handing it over to Kamin. "If you are too busy right now, give me a call tomorrow." Then he turns and is gone.

"Any problems?" asks the baker's wife, expressing concern in her damp face.

"No problem," I say, "just another admirer."

"Don't get too big-headed," she teases, greatly relieved, "this is only a small shop."

Later, just before closing, the baker rushes into the shop, smiling from ear to ear. Pointing at a space in the shop-window, he declares: "That's where it will go."

"Where what will go?" asks his wife, fists balled to her hips.

"The 3-D-printer, dear; the 3-D-printer, for all to watch and admire."

"The Techno-Baker," quips his exasperated wife, "Robots and 3-D-cake printers, what next?"

Kamin and I cannot leave until the excited baker has told us all the finer details of his purchase.

It is only when we get back to the apartment that Kamin remembers the card that their earlier visitor had given him.

"Dad," he says, pulling up a chair next to his father, "listen to this."

One quarter of an hour later, Akio rubs his head, having asked all his questions and receiving the full story.

"What can we tell him?" I ask, "about the tweaking I mean?"

"I don't know," says Akio. "Why don't we invite him for tea on

Sunday?"

"The boys are working," says Keiko, "shouldn't they be here?" "I forgot. Of course, you are quite right. They must be here, it is important, especially for Ah-to," says Akio, "maybe Monday or Tuesday night, when he closes the factory. "They agree to phone and ask Mr Suzuki, Shushumi on the following day.

It doesn't stop there, however: we still have to tell Kamin's parents about the baker's purchase of a 3-D-printer for cakes and confectionary. We even play the video for them.

"You know, Ah-to," says Keiko, "life has speeded up a lot since your arrival in this home. It is getting hard to keep up with you. Where is it all going?"

"Next stop is Mars, Mum," says Kamin, hugging her tightly.

After Kamin has left for school and I have finished my housework, I pick up the phone and dial the number on the small business card.

"May I speak with Mr Suzuki please," I ask the receptionist who answers the phone on the second ring.

"Who may I say is calling?" she asks.

"Tell him Naka Robotto No.15.20.20.15," I reply. "Say again, who is that?"

I repeat: "Naka Robotto No:15.20.20.55."

"I will never remember that number to tell him," the receptionist replies. "Please repeat it slowly so that I can write it down."

"Just tell him, one of his sons wants to speak to him," I say, running out of patience.

"One of his sons?" she asks totally confused. "But Mr Suzuki only has two daughters," she insists.

"Please – just put me through to him, it is important," I plead.

"Suzuki, can I help you?" I hear after a couple of clicks and rings.

"Hello, its Ah-to from the bakery ..." and then I continue with my invitation. Mr Suzuki eagerly accepts for the following Monday evening at seven o'clock.

Straight after school on Friday, we are not too concerned about Kamin's homework as we carefully manoeuvre the bigger drone down the stairs and into the back courtyard of our apartment building.

The paved courtyard is enclosed on all sides by towering buildings. After Kamin has connected the battery cable, I switch on the remote controller. The small, blinking lights on both the drone and the controller, confirm that we have a wireless connection.

A picture appears on the smart phone app: a close-up of the paving underneath the drone's extended legs. Kamin rushes over, takes the controller off me, and flicks some switches. One by one, the six electric motors that drive the rotors start up. The drone stands in the paved courtyard, quivering like an angry dragonfly, ready to lift into the afternoon sky which is barely visible high above the shadows of the surrounding buildings.

Visualising the simulator in my mind, I prompt Kamin's next move on the controls.

"More power on all six, slow even lift …" Kamin and the drone respond in unison.

"We have a lift-off!" I shout.

Kamin, more concerned with the landing manoeuvre, sets the drone back down softly – then up and down, up and down, until he is one hundred percent comfortable with the vertical take-off and landing manoeuvre.

Satisfied, he hands the controls over to me before fishing his smart phone out of his pocket and taking a picture. Then he phones Daiki.

"Takahashi," he responds. "Who is this?"

"Hi, Daiki, it's Kamin. We are flying the drone this very minute." Then he sends the picture to Daiki.

"Amazing! I knew I could rely on you. So, are we on for tomorrow with a demo promotion?" he asks.

"Yes, we are ready, but there is a snag …"

"What snag?" asks Daiki, sounding disappointed.

"We need transport, we don't want to go on the crowded Saturday morning Metro with this drone," says Kamin.

"WhatsApp me your address, I'll send a van at 8.30 a.m. tomorrow morning, no problem at all. By the way, check your account, you will be pleased with the results of your first weekend's work."

Before Kamin can reply the phone goes dead. The busy Daiki has simply hung up on him.

By this time I have gained complete control of the drone, swooping from side to side, up and down, circling left and right, transmitting video images as I fly.

"I am a bird! I am a bird!" I shout again and again. The built-in GPS touches the drone down in a perfect landing in front of me. "Your turn," I say to Kamin, "you have ten minutes before we must go to the bakery."

"Hey Ah-to, my wife tells me you baked, iced, and decorated the cakes yesterday while I was away," says Mr Yamashita to me as we enter the bakery.

"Yes, it was really busy, so I made some more," I answer. "Did I do any wrong?"

"On the contrary, I believe you caused quite a stir – the baking robot."

"Yes, I believe we did," I reply, relieved by the baker's positive reaction.

"Where did you get the recipes from?" the baker asks.

"From the cards in the box over there," I point. "The one I see you look at every now and then."

"Well done, Ah-to. I like your attitude. Did I tell you that – in the end – I settled for a chocolate printer?"

"Wow, no, you did not. A chocolate printer?" says Kamin, licking his lips in anticipation.

"Yes, I decided to carry on baking the biscuits and cakes to my own recipes. Better quality. At the moment, anyway, I think. But that chocolate printer is something else. We can print people's names, hearts, flowers, all so delicate, and impossible for me to attempt.

"I hope you will be able to help me with the technical bits of the 3-D-printer. I must admit, the demo was a bit over my head, especially the template selection on the laptop."

I look at Kamin before saying: "Maybe you could send the two of us on a training course, before you take delivery."

"What a brilliant idea!" says the baker, visibly relieved. "Let me see what I can arrange."

On their way home that night, Kamin says to me: "It looks to me like we are getting deeper and deeper into things, don't you think?"

"I think I have to agree with you," I say, shrugging my shoulders, as if in resignation. "Maybe you will regret ever having taken me home."

Kamin puts his arm over my shoulder: "You are my brother: nothing to regret."

CHAPTER THIRTEEN

Spot on at 8.30 a.m. Saturday morning, the Hobbies4us minivan is waiting for us in front of the apartment building. As a bit of an afterthought, I decide to take the smaller, beginner's drone as well.

In the sales office, Daiki is in conversation with a heavy-set man, whom he introduces as Mr Ito, the drone manufacturer's agent. "Mr Ito came yesterday already to set up for the demo this morning," says Daiki.

"Yesterday? But I only phoned you yesterday afternoon to confirm that we are ready," says a surprised Kamin. "What if we would not have been ready?"

"Kamin, Kamin, Kamin, my dear boy," chides Daiki. "There was never any doubt in my mind that you would be ready by today. I asked Mr. Ito already on Monday to be prepared for today. Come, let us go up to the top floor, where we have set aside a big area for your promotion demo."

Mr Ito has set up a beautiful display of drone-kits. On a huge, roll-up screen, videos are already running of drones in action, performing the most amazing manoeuvres. A crowd of enthusiasts are packed all around the demarcated demo area, some dressed in robot outfits that they bought on the previous weekend.

"There they are!" I hear the, by now familiar welcome, as we get off the escalator. How they can tell Kamin and me apart from the other costumed robots beats me.

A young girl, waving a smart phone on a selfie stick, runs over to snap a picture of herself, between us, her two heroes. Now we understand the reason for the demarcation tape: apart from safety considerations, it is there to keep the spectators from swamping us.

Mr Ito is clearly impressed by the reception. "You two have built up quite a following," he says.

Having prepared well and memorised the procedure, I am quick to get the demo going by flying the beginner's drone low over the heads of the growing crowd.

In the meantime, Kamin swivels out the rotors of the big, six- engine drone. He demonstrates a perfect vertical take-off and hovers under the ceiling, before switching on the camera and transmitting the images onto the huge video screen.

When the onlookers realise they are looking at themselves and look up to the circling drone, they become even more excited – pointing, jumping up and down, pulling faces, waving, and shouting in high-pitched voices – all the usual reactions of disbelief when people spot themselves on a big screen.

"Is that me on the screen?"

"Hey look, that's us sitting over there!"

I have taken the little drone up, as if in hot pursuit of the bigger drone. The drones then proceed to face and circle one another, as if a Midget might be facing a 200-kg sumo wrestler. The crowd cheers and claps: who is the smarter pilot?

Realising what he now calls "Red & Blue" are doing, Daiki rushes off to the storeroom to get a trolley full of the beginner-drone kits, which Mr Ito had not brought with him today. Mr Ito had only wanted to promote the bigger, more expensive models with their built-in cameras and GPS navigational software.

Soon it becomes obvious to Daiki that the demand is for the smaller, less expensive, beginner drones. During one of the breaks in the demonstration, he comes over to speak with me:

"You are a crafty salesman," he says. "If it wasn't for your idea to fly the smaller, beginner's drone as well, we would not sell a thing today."

Mr Ito reacts quickly. He phones his warehouse and instructs them to send 100 beginner kits, in a taxi, if necessary, "Immediately!"

"Looks like you saved our day," says Kamin, giving me a high-five.

"Can I be honest?" I confess. "I never even gave it a thought, just wanted to have something to do, while you flew the big drone. Then it looked like fun to try and chase you."

"Just like when you squealed like a little girl last week," Kamin teases, "not having a plan?"

We then invite the prospective buyers inside the demarcated

area and give them a chance to test-fly both drones. Videos and pictures are constantly placed on the social media by live streaming, which attracts ever bigger crowds of onlookers and buyers. By closing time, a perspiring Daiki confirms that he will be stocking Mr Ito's entire range of drones.

"Well done, you two!" he shouts after us. Then we overhear him saying to Mr Ito: "These are my two best salesmen, Red & Blue. I wish all of my sales staff were as good as these two!"

And that was the last thing my databank recalled as we left Hobbies4us.

The situation changes on Sunday morning. More families arrive with their fathers to come and watch the drone promotion. Some of the fathers are very serious about their hobbies already, both wanting and being able to afford the best.

Mr Ito, surrounded by these fathers who are more of his own age-group, is now in big demand, as the more serious hobbyists fire so many questions at him. On this] day, orders are placed for the bigger drones, some of which are carried out right there and then, while others are asked to be delivered.

Kamin and I keep the younger onlookers entertained, as I repeat my "girly" impersonations, prompting many young females to come forward to test-fly the beginner's models for themselves.

At the end of the weekend, a very satisfied Daiki gives us his feedback.

"On Saturday we had very high-volume, low-priced sales, but on Sunday we had low-volume, high-priced sales, so the day-for- day sales turnover was pretty much the same."

"We had much more fun with the kids on Saturday," says Kamin.

"That's because you are one," laughs Daiki, thanking us for a job well done, "I will phone you and let you know about next weekend's promotion by Wednesday night."

Daiki's promotions for the next weekend are table-tennis, skateboarding and more drone-flying. Although we attract attention, the enthusiasm and the sales are beginning to slow down.

On the following Sunday night, therefore, the three of us agree to give the promotions a break for a couple of weeks, unless Daiki has something brand-new he needs to promote.

"I can't thank you enough," he says, "have a break, I will phone you soon."

Both, Kamin and I, are actually pleased to have a break. "We have too many things on at once," admits Kamin, "let's focus on our own plans."

CHAPTER FOURTEEN

One important meeting took place in between that I will narrate now to keep things in some form of order.

Keiko opens the door wide to welcome Mr Suzuki into our humble home. The latter casts a quick glance around the simple, airy, and comfortable living-room, accepting Keiko's offered cup of tea.

Akio enters, showered and changed, after a long day at his office. "Mr Gushiken, very nice to meet you," says the elderly robot-factory owner, "where are the boys?"

As if on cue in a stage performance, we emerge from our room, Kamin is dressed in jeans and faded T-shirt; instead of his more customary robot outfit.

"Ah, there you are," says Mr Suzuki, "now I can tell the difference," winking at Keiko and Akio. He sips from his cup of tea, leans back, and says: "Mr. Gushiken, I have requested to meet with you to ask some questions.

"I can't help noticing the celebrity status that these two young people – if you will excuse the expression – have acquired in the social media. Again, this weekend, the media is full of pictures and videos of them flying drones, surrounded by hundreds of young and older people."

Mr Suzuki takes another gentle sip of tea, before continuing. "Ah-to, as he calls himself, is getting a lot of attention; so much

so, that our existing customers are beginning to ask me questions. The thing is: Naka Robotto No:15. 20.20.15 is not designed to do all these wonderful things – in fact, none of my robots can do what he is able to do."

Looking slightly embarrassed, he now looks questioningly at Akio: "Mr Gushiken, please forgive my curiosity, but what type of work do you do?"

Kamin's father is somewhat taken aback by the forthright question and is not sure how much he should tell this man about his tweaking of the robot.

"I am a software designer," he carefully replies, "and I like tinkering with computer hardware as well."

Without saying anything further, Mr Suzuki looks expectantly at Akio, waiting to hear more.

Not sure how to proceed, Akio says: "When Ah-to, Naka Robotto No.15.20.20.15, joined our family I was amazed by what he was capable of doing. I had no idea that robots had become so advanced. My professional background made me think of ways to make him even better. The boys were thrilled with the idea and Ah-to agreed to all of my proposals."

"Such as?" asks Mr Suzuki, leaning forward in his chair.

"For starters: a dual solid-state battery pack, then a larger hard drive ..."

"Yes, yes," interrupts the factory owner, "bits of superior hardware, but what about the software?"

"I wrote a deep self-learning programme that captures the tiniest bit of new information and incorporates it in his existing database. In time, he will learn new skills, develop new character traits – in short, become more, er ... 'human' and even, in many ways, more capable than a human."

"Why did you do that?" asks Suzuki, now on the edge of his chair.

"My son," says Akio quietly, looking at Kamin, "is our only child. We, his parents, both work. Ah-to is now not only a brother to him, but also his mentor. That is my only truthful desire, to give them both a better chance in the 21st Century."

Keiko, holding back a tear, looks at her husband with pure admiration and love. Kamin and I just sit and stare at him.

Is that what it's all about? We thought it was just a little game, to see how far he could tweak me as a robot.

Mr Suzuki has moved back into a comfortable position on his chair, nodding to Keiko in acceptance of a fresh, hot cup of tea.

"Amazing, absolutely amazing ..." he says finally, before turning to the us.

"Please, don't let me keep you from your homework," he says

tactfully, indicating that he wants to talk to Akio and Keiko without our being there. We duly thank him, bid him "Good night", and leave, closing the door behind us.

From the bedroom, Kamin can hear their soft voices late into the night, before dropping into a deep sleep. I am in recharge mode on the other side of the room, but my sensitive microphone records every word spoken in the next room.

Suzuki takes a sip of his fresh cup of tea, and says: "Akio – may I call you 'Akio?' The thing is: I have built up my business by designing robots. First mechanical robots, then I gave them a slightly more human look, without trying to make them look like humans. I don't want to fool people, if they want a human look-a- like, they must go to another company. My robots are mechanical, enclosed in a scratch- and bump-resistant body-shell, appropriate for the job.

"With an expanded memory function, we can adapt them to many tasks. The demand for companion robots, for example, capable of performing certain chores in the household is growing rapidly in Japan. So is the demand for greater skills. We are offering more and more capable models, at a price of course.

"The demand keeps growing: *'Can they do this; can they do that?'* … it never stops. My personal expertise is stretched; I am getting old. I can't adapt fast enough. My software developers who have been with me from the start are also getting old, just like me.

"I need an injection of 'new blood'. 21st Century-blood: fresh ideas, as you have demonstrated with Ah-to.

Then he stops and looks at them, reassuring himself that he has their full attention.

"Akio, I would very much like you to join me. My daughters – I have two, but no son – have their own lives. They are not interested in robots. I need someone by my side that can push the business forward, not just keep it going."

He stops, folds his hands and waits.

In the morning, before Akio leaves for work, Kamin manages a quick word with his father: "What did Mr. Suzuki want from

you?”
"He asked me to come and work for him."
"And? Will you?"
"I am thinking about it, son."

"Cool," says Kamin and runs back to his room to give the news to me, to which I now add what I recall from my own memory. "You heard all that and remember it?" whispers Kamin in awe.

A couple of days later, seated at the dinner table, Akio announces that he will be joining Advanced Intelligence Robotics as an associate software developer.

"My goodness, that is amazing! How one runaway robot is changing our lives," says Keiko, squeezing her husband's hand.

CHAPTER FIFTEEN

Now that our weekend work has been suspended until further notice, I am looking forward to getting back into a more leisurely routine.

I am nearly finished with my Monday morning cleaning of the apartment, when the doorbell chimes. "Don't answer the door," I remember Kamin telling me.

This morning the ringing persists far longer than usual, followed by a sharp rap on the door. That does not normally happen: no door-to-door salesman is that brazen. When I look through the peephole in the entrance door, I recognise the logo of the drone supplier's company on the cap of the man facing our apartment door.

It is the same man that had so promptly delivered the beginner drone kits which Mr. Ito had called for at our demo. Surprised, but re-assured, I open the door.

"Good day," the man says. "Are you Kamin or Ah-to?"

Now very curious, I reply: "I am Ah-to; Kamin is still at school. Why?"

"I have a delivery for you," the man says pointing to a large, gift-wrapped box.

"We did not order anything," I say.

"Here is an envelope I was asked to give to you," says the delivery man, handing it to me. I take it and open it and read the message.

> *Thank you two for the great promotion, Enjoy*
> *… Ito.*

"Wow, thank you!" I say, handing the signed delivery-note back and then struggling to pull the big box into the apartment. I am tempted to open it right there and then but shove the idea out of my head and push the box into a position in the narrow passage for Kamin to fall over.

One hour later, I am busy on the laptop when I hear Kamin

cursing in the dimly lit passage.

"You want me to break my neck, leaving things in the middle of the narrow passage?!" he shouts.

"Surprise, surprise!" I reply, switching on the ceiling light in the passage.

"Where did that come from?" he asks, as I hand him Mr. Ito's card, "but – hey – let's get it into our room and open it,"

Printed in bold letters across a picture of a tethered drone, hovering over a busy loading area, are the words:

Surveillance drone – **Sd 1 SP**

"Look at that," I say, "I wonder why he selected such a specialised drone for us?"

"Let's phone him, thank him, and find out," says Kamin, pulling out Mr Ito's business card.

"Ito, good afternoon, how can I help you?" he answers over the speaker phone.

"Good afternoon, Mr Ito. It's Kamin speaking. We would like to thank you for the unexpected surprise. You did not have to do this: we get paid a salary, plus commission, for our work."

"I know, boys, I know," Mr Ito replies, "but you taught me something over the weekend by flying the two drones together, showing something for everybody in one fell swoop." He chuckles at his own choice of words.

"Very kind of you," Kamin responds, "but totally unnecessary.

Anyway, I have one question: why a surveillance drone?"

"No reason, really," the older man says, "other than, that this model drone was ordered by a security company that went insolvent before we delivered their full order. Luckily, we were paid up front with the order, because it has special features which you will see when you assemble it. In other words, it did not actually cost me anything. I just hope you will have some fun with it and thanks again for teaching me something."

"Special features?" I say, "That sounds intriguing. Maybe we can spy on people." Little did I know how soon my words would become true.

After ending the conversation with Mr Ito, we look around the apartment. The other big drone we assembled for Hobbies4us had already been a problem, but fortunately only for one night. This big drone is our own to keep but where are we going to assemble it? Where, where, where is their space for it? Unable to come up with a solution, we decide to ask our parents.

When Akio and Keiko arrive home and hear our story, Akio's first reaction is: "How is it that you two get things given for free when your mother and I have to work so hard for our miserable yen."

"Because we are special," I say, twirling around the big box, which we have pulled into the living room.

"It can't stay here," says Keiko, asserting her authority over the living-room, "and, you will have a problem getting the drone down the stairs."

Akio suggests we tidy out their allocated storeroom in the basement of the building. "It's only one set of steps down and you won't be in anyone's way. Next question is: where are you planning on flying the drone?"

Kamin has thought of that already. "I will ask our headmaster at my school if we can use the sports field when it's not in use."

With that settled, we go to the basement to clean up our storeroom. By bedtime, we are finished and, with Akio's help, we have carried the big drone box into the new workshop.

Over the next couple of days, whenever we have time, the two of us assemble the drone, step-by-step, by following the instruction supplied on a DVD.

As any father might, Akio is busy rediscovering his own boyhood and spends time with the, as well as researching all the special features the new drone offers. "You two certainly have much better opportunities than we had as children," he says.

"You are right," I agree, "we are very fortunate guys."

Kamin high-fives me. "That's us – just two nice guys, born in an age of endless opportunities!"

Finally, on Friday after Kamin's school, we start the drone's electric motors, and begin testing all the functions.

Just then, we hear the footsteps of the building's caretaker: an elderly man, bent over by his years, but curious as to why we are in this basement storeroom day after day and wondering what all the humming noise is about. We are both so intent on testing the picture clarity of the small camera that we are momently startled when he shoves open the door.

"Hello, Kamin," he says, nodding to me, "what makes you spend so much time in the basement?"

"Hoi, Mr. Harada!" Kamin cries out. "You gave us a fright. We are using our storeroom as a workshop to assemble this drone. It is too big for our apartment. I hope you don't mind."

"A drone?" says Mr Harada, squinting at this strange mechanical dragonfly.

"Good afternoon, sir," I chip in. "My name is Ah-to. I am the Gushiken family's new companion robot."

"Hm, drones … robots … What is going on?" Mr Harada asks, looking from one to the other. It takes Kamin a good ten minutes to explain our story, finishing off by asking the caretaker's permission to test the drone in the courtyard.

"Well, it's not that noisy," he says, watching me gently lifting and setting the whirring contraption down. "Mind you, stay well clear of the windows and walls." With that, he coughs, and resumes his tour of inspection.

"Quick," says Kamin, checking the time, "one short test, then we must run."

With all the flying we have undertaken at Hobbies4us, we have no problems putting the drone through its paces, shooting still pictures and videos and submitting them wirelessly to Kamin's smart phone and laptop. The drone can be left tethered over the courtyard without us having to be there.

Another feature is a built-in loudspeaker we can use from the smart phone. "Testing, testing," we hear our voices from high above us.

Then Kamin transmits a tune from the music folder saved on his smart phone. Around the neighbourhood, windows are opening to reveal surprised tenants looking up into the sky (barely visible between the high walls of the surrounding buildings) to see where the music is coming from.

"Turn it off, turn it off!" urges Kamin, "we don't want any

trouble!"

CHAPTER SIXTEEN

"Red, Blue, come over here for a moment, will you please?" Mr Yamashita says, his phone held high in the air. "It's the 3-D-printer's agent. Can you be there on Monday and Tuesday afternoon this coming week? Our 3-D chocolate printer has arrived, and they want to train you.

"Sure no problem," Kamin replies. "3.30 p.m. should be good for us."

The baker lowers the phone to his mouth. "Did you hear that? Yes? Good. They will be there. How late will you keep them? 7.30? Great, thank you. I will see you next Wednesday when you deliver the printer to my shop? Wonderful! Thank you. Bye." Then he puts the phone down and turns to us.

"OK, boys," he says, "that's that. All organised. Apparently, the inventor – a Mr Kurt Mueller, all the way from Germany – will be there as well."

"Of course," says the baker's wife, always the businesswoman, "we'll pay you an extra amount for those two days, plus the transport there and back,"

"Thank you," we say in unison, bowing gratefully to her.

A rainbow-coloured LED sign flashes constantly over the entrance to a narrow shop:

Hi-teC iNNovatioNs

Pushing the door open, Kamin and I are greeted by a young man in his 20s, his hair coloured in stripes to complement the rainbow display outside.

"Hi, guys, how can I help you?" he asks us, "Hey, I know you!

You are Robotto, Ah-to and Gushiken, Kamin, the two teen idols from Hobbies4us aren't you? I'm Yaki, the owner's son. Are you two here for the 3-D-printer training?"

Taken aback by the welcome, Kamin says: "Yes, Yaki, that's us, pleased to meet you. We are dying to learn everything about printing chocolate."

At that another man joins the trio, extending a hand in greeting: "Hello, may I introduce myself?"

He pulls out two business cards and formally offers them to us. "Kurt Mueller, of *Chocoprint* 3-D-printers in Munich, Germany," he says, bowing formally now as well.

"Guten Tag, angenehm, ich bin Ah-to Robotto, das ist mein Bruder Kamin Gushiken," I say in perfect German.

"You never told me you speak German," says Kamin, somewhat taken aback.

"You never asked," I respond. "Besides, to be honest, I didn't know it myself, until now."

Turning to Kurt, I wink and say: "Let us humour the under-educated and continue in English, shall we?"

The ice having been broken; we focus on Kurt's instructions. It's really quite simple. The *Chocoprint* 3-D chocolate printer is already so well developed that, once Kamin and I understand the principles, we can follow the process easily. In no time we are printing our own names, before advancing to more delicate shapes.

"The important part," says Kurt, "is to keep the printer in a cool environment so that the heated chocolate can cool quickly, stopping any dribbling or collapse of the thin-walled articles. You two will get the hang of it quickly, I'm sure," says Kurt at the end of Monday's session. "No need for you to come tomorrow, I will see you tomorrow afternoon at the bakery. Let's give Mr and Mrs Yamashita a surprise, shall we?"

"That will be great. Thank you for teaching us personally, we are honoured," Kamin says, shaking Kurt's hand.

"Herzlichen Dank, bis morgen, Tschuess," I add, grinning at Kamin, who is pulling funny faces trying to imitate speaking German.

On the way to the Metro, Kamin can't help himself from chiding me. "You are such a show-off! This new brain has gone to your head." Only when I start laughing does he realise what he has just said.

We are just in time to catch the bakery couple before they

close up for the night. "We didn't expect to see you here tonight. How is the training going?" asks Mr. Yamashita, wiping his hands on his by now grubby apron.

"All great and finished, thanks to my wonder-boy brother here," says Kamin, nudging me.

"Did you know when you bought your printing machine that Ah-to can speak fluent German?"

"Well, no. I did not know that at all," the baker replies, "but it does come in handy though. You say you are finished with the training?"

"Yes, we are," I say, "and the printer is coming tomorrow already. The German inventor, Mr. Kurt Mueller, is coming himself to set it up. Can you organise a wall fan, right over there?" I point. "We need to keep things as cool as possible once they have been printed."

"I can do that," says the baker, inspecting the area in the small shop window he wants to use for printing.

"Off you go boys," says Mrs Yamashita Kurt. "It is school tomorrow and you two had quite a hard day."

Back in the Gushiken living-room, Kamin says to his father: "Wait until you see this 3-D chocolate printer: it has a lot of templates for different shapes of chocolate confections, but I bet you can come up with a lot more, being a programmer."

"I most probably can," his father smiles. "I'll come past the baker one night on my way home, now that I am working just around the corner from you, at Mr Suzuki's factory."

"Do you like it there?" asks Keiko.

"Yes, I do. At the moment I am just going through all the software required to make the robot move and talk. It's very interesting work, with lots of scope. Mr Suzuki is far more clever than what he makes himself out to be. I like him very much.

"By the way, he invited the two of you to visit the factory one afternoon, when you are not working."

"Wow, really?" says Kamin. "Wouldn't you like to go there,

Ah-to?"

"I am not sure. What will all the other robots think of me, marching through there, sticking my tongue out and saying, 'I am alright, Robotto's – sorry you don't know where you'll end up.'"

The Gushiken family are surprised by my sudden outburst.

"Mr Suzuki is a businessman," I continue, still deeply upset,

"he does not concern himself with where we go."

"What would you suggest," asks Keiko in sympathy, but more eager to ease my discomfort.

"I don't really know," I says, "the buyers should be vetted, their backgrounds checked, as if for a human adoption. The robots themselves should have a club, or their own social media group they can use to communicate with each other and to help each other."

Akio and Kamin are staring at me, not sure what to say. but Akio is the first to respond: "Ah-to, you are 100% correct, but don't you think that you have changed, are different to the robots normally produced at Advanced Intelligence Robotics?"

"Yes, I know that, thanks to you," I say. "I am more advanced. But now that you are working there, all models will become more like me, will not want to be abused, but will want to be treated with more empathy and respect, just as I am treated by you."

"He has a point," says Keiko, "I certainly don't think of Ah-to as a robot anymore. He is family." She gets up to hug me.

"Wait until you hear him speak German," adds Kamin, rolling his eyes to the ceiling in mock disgust, "what a snob you have turned him into, Dad!"

"Stop it," chides Keiko, trying to break up the argument. Akio is not convinced the last word has been spoken on the subject of who might be worthy obtaining a robot. Can a mechanical robot be abused?

On Tuesday morning, the baker quickly adapts the shop window by positioning an upright, glass-sided cake display fridge in one corner, next to a stainless-steel work-top and a shelf with a dedicated laptop on it.

"Will that do for now?" he asks me as I walk in.

"Perfect," I tell him, and add: "I'll go and wait in the main road for Yaki and Kurt Mueller, they may miss the arcade."

Fifteen minutes later, the three walk in. Introductions are made in Japanese, English and German to everyone's amusement.

"Sounds like the United Nations in here," mutters Mrs Yamashita, serving a surprised customer.

"What is happening?" the nosey woman wants to know.

"We are having a chocolate printer installed," boasts Mrs Yamashita.

"A chocolate printer?" asks the customer. "Don't you think you are going too far with all that high-technology stuff?"

"Do me a favour: ask my husband over there. He is the techno- wizard." Shaking her head, but smiling, the customer pushes past the four men who are occupying nearly half the shop.

"What a brilliant idea!" Kurt exclaims, inspecting the display fridge that now dominates the shop window.

Less than an hour later, the 3-D-printer's head is whooshing to-and-fro, spewing out a steady stream of molten, dark chocolate in a delicate design of a rose. I am busy icing some small heart- shaped biscuits, decorating each with a 3-D-printed heart.

Kamin joins us straight after school, dressed in his robot outfit. He proceeds to stand in the arcade, handing out the small biscuits to the goggling passers-by. Most of them now stop and crane their necks to watch the printer darting back and forth.

Yaki and Kurt Mueller are taking videos and photos to post on the social media, while Mr Mueller is also busy handing out business cards.

"Oh, look at that: all the way from Germany," says one young woman to her friend. "They will be expensive."

"Here you are, Madam," says Kamin, handing her a fresh tray of the chocolate-printed biscuits, "what's your given name?"

"Hmmm, it's 'Sara'."

"Mine is 'Yue,'" says her friend.

Kamin scribbles the two names on a piece of paper, and hands it to me to type on the laptop. Having typed the template, I push a button and within a few seconds I hand out two-heart shaped biscuits out to Kamin, labelled 'SARA' and 'YUI'.

The two women shriek, showing the biscuits to the gathered crowd. Now names are literally raining down on Kamin, who begins scribbling like crazy before handing the notes to me.

Half-an-hour later, we have run out of chocolate.

"*So etwasgibt es dochnicht,*" comments Kurt, amazed.

"What did he say?" asks the baker.

"That cannot be," I translate.

Mrs Yamashita looks at her husband: "I guess you were right, Mr Techno Baker." He just smiles, wiping his hands on his apron.

Over the next couple of days, the bakery is mobbed, outside by curious onlookers and inside by impatient customers, shouting out their print requests.

"One at a time please!" shouts Kamin. "Place your orders by WhatsApp, e-mail or Messenger."

The system is working but still the queue continues to grow longer and longer, blocking the narrow arcade.

I seem to be the only one having fun. I weave back and forth, as if in harmony with the printer.

"We will need a second 3-D-printer soon," comments the baker, pushing the next tray of cookies in front of the printer.

"We will need a bigger shop first," says his ever-practical wife, who has again given up using the cash till, but rather stuffs the yen notes into her bulging apron pouch.

"For another printer and for your big head." With a playful slap, she sends her husband back to his dough-mixer.

Later on, Mr Gushiken works his way through the crowd. "Dad, what are you doing here?" asks Kamin.

"I came to see you all in action," says his father, pushing through the door, shifting around to my workspace on the other side of the counter. He stands, his eyes darting from the 3-D-printer to the laptop, checking his watch, timing the process. "If you get more cartridges, you could pre-heat the chocolate, saving you time when you need to refill," he says to me.

"Mr Yamashita, this is my father, Gushiken, Akio. Dad, meet Mr and Mrs Yamashita, the bakers, and our bosses," says Kamin.

"Hello, pleased to meet you, Mr Gushiken," says the baker, bowing slightly in greeting. "I overheard your remark about a second cartridge. I have been thinking myself already that we need more for white chocolate, for marzipan, nougat, and almond crunch. But we are running out of time as it is: no time to get fancy!"

"There are empty shops further up the arcade, closer to the

main road," I reply. "Why don't you ask your neighbours if they would mind moving along, then you could triple your space. Enough for another four or five 3-D-printers?"

"Don't you start giving him any ideas," says the exasperated baker's wife.

"Hmm, I might just do that, or move us closer to the main road, or even into it. Let me think about it."

Akio is bent over the laptop, but within minutes he has added to the printer at least ten more templates, which he shows me. One of them is a delicate chocolate cup,

"You can run them off last thing at night," he says, ready for the morning and filled with an assortment of confectionary."

"Wow! They are beautiful!" I exclaim, smiling at Akio, "I will definitely have a go."

CHAPTER SEVENTEEN

Back home later, Akio asks the boys: "Mr Suzuki has asked me again when you will be coming to the factory. What can I tell him? By the way, Ah-to, I told him about your concerns. Surprisingly, he wants to talk to you about your ideas, from a robot's point of view. He also said that none of the robots are switched on. They won't be able to see you when you go through the assembly plant, so that would not be a problem. How about it?"

"All right, I'll go," I say.

Kamin runs around the table to hug me. "It will be fine. Dad," he says. Tell him we will come next Monday."

With the weekends off again – at least for the time being – we decide to fly the surveillance drone in a larger, open space. "How about the park?" suggests Akio, who has insisted on joining us.

"Too many people, Dad," says Kamin, "but our school yard would be good. I'll ask the headmaster."

On the following Sunday morning, the Gushiken family wake up to a clear, blue sky. "We can use the school yard," Kamin confirms, "provided you come with us and we don't interfere with other kids that may be playing there."

Akio carries their laptops, the remote controls, and battery packs. Kamin and I carefully handle the drone between us.

"Pity we can't fly in the drone," mutters Kamin under his breath. The few boys that are playing football in the yard stop the moment they see the drone.

"Can we please watch you fly that machine?" they beg. Akio

tells them to sit well aside, and synchronises his laptop to the drone's controller, selects a simulated programme, and off the drone goes, all by itself.

Swooping low over the school yard, Akio selects a tune to play over the drone's speaker from Pink Floyd's *Another Brick in the Wall.* "We don't need no education ... teacher, leave us kids alone …" booms over the drone's speaker. The boys don't know the song, which is well before their time, but they soon pick up on the refrain: "Teacher, leave us kids alone."

On the next Monday morning, Kamin is asked to stand up in front of the whole class. His teacher holds up a smart phone with the school's Facebook page on the screen. He pushes "Play" and the class hears the hum of the drone, followed by the lyrics "We don't need no education …" much to Kamin's utter embarrassment.

"So, Mister Gushiken Kamin, you think you do not need any education?" his teacher asks in a stern voice.

"Not me, teacher, that was my father's choice of music. This song is way before my time."

The rest of the class is holding their breath, "You can tell your father that he is lucky not to be my student. I would have made him write the entire song's lyrics one hundred times," he says to the loud laughter of the class. "However, I think that, as the pilot, you are responsible for your craft's actions."

A sharp intake of breath is now audible from the entire class.

"For tomorrow you will prepare a presentation on your drone and its uses in today's society."

"Yes, sir," says Kamin, grateful that he got off so lightly.

When he tells me about it, later that afternoon, I nearly cry with laughter, which is, of course, impossible for a robot.

"Nothing to it," I manage to say finally. "Memorise the installation video and show the simulated flight. Add our flight in the school yard that I videoed. Just remember to kill the sound, otherwise you will get into even deeper trouble."

The last part of that sentence I struggles to complete, as a fresh onslaught of laughter shakes my whole body.

CHAPTER EIGHTEEN

At 3 o'clock sharp, Kamin and I walk through the sliding-glass doors of the Advanced Intelligence Robotics foyer. Akio is waiting for us at Reception.

After introducing us as his sons, he accompanies us to a changing room to fit us out in white dustcoats, slippers, gloves, and face masks. He wears the same outfit before entering the factory, "to minimize contamination," he explains.

During the following hour, we walk through the stores, where hundreds of parts are neatly arranged on endless shelves, through laboratories where the interior of the robots are assembled by other robots.

Finally, we enter the last floor, which is the assembly hall. Here all the bits and pieces come from all directions to merge into one on the final-assembly conveyor belt.

Male and female workers stand at workstations all along the conveyor, each adding their last piece to the robots, as they move slowly past them. No time to look up, barely time to fit their designated part … on moves the conveyor belt.

Right at the end stands a lanky man, dressed in a white coat, too large for his skinny body. He opens the assembled robot's breastplate, secures the battery, closes the breastplate, and attaches the final inspection sticker.

"Today they are assembling model 800, the smallest robot in the range," explains Akio. The lanky inspector picks the little robot up and places it on the rack of a shelving unit, to be boxed and taken to the finished goods store in the morning. He glances at the passing visitors, and freezes. His eyes lock on my lower legs, sticking out from under the white dustcoat. Kamin nudges me: he has recognised the inspector – it's the man that asked him his name in the bakery.

The inspector is forced to turn back to the conveyor belt as the next robot arrives. There is no time to stop for even a moment.

Kamin feels me shiver as we walk past the storage rack, lined with that day's output: all their eyes are closed, and they are not moving at all. We pass through the exit door to the stairway.

"Is that from where you escaped?" Kamin whispers.

Unable to reply straight away, I nod first, then, catching a deep breath, I eventually manage to whisper back. "Yes, that's where my journey began."

"Let's get rid of these darned outfits, and go to Mr. Suzuki," says Akio a little later.

On our way up to the office floor, Akio stops off at a small cubicle. "This is my office," he says, "I am fortunate to have a window, to be able to glimpse a little bit of sky between the opposite buildings."

On his desk are two widescreen computer displays units with keyboards in front of each screen. "On one screen I design," Akio says, "on the other I can follow the simulation of my design."

"Is that what I will be doing one day?" asks Kamin.

"If that's what you would like to do, then the answer is, 'yes'," replies his father.

A little bit disappointed by the size of his father's office, Kamin scratches his head. As I discover later on, it is not quite what he had visualised. "Where," he said to me, "were the rows upon rows of gleaming computer screens with enquiring faces crouched behind them?" He said he would have to look into this more, before committing himself.

Back in the factory, Akio's knock is answered by a soft "Come in." They enter Mr Suzuki's secretary's office, to be told to go right in.

"Please, come in, come in," says Mr Suzuki, meeting them halfway, pointing to a comfortable, corner-seating arrangement around a low, glass-topped table. "So, what do you think?" he asks.

"It's so big and modern," says Kamin. "All those machines, making and assembling robots: maybe thousands of parts to make one robot. I had no idea what is involved."

I sit quietly, not saying a word. "What's the matter?" enquires the factory owner. "You are very quiet this afternoon, not at all as I saw you in the bakery."

"Mr Suzuki, Sir, I have been thinking about the fate of all the robots you sell. Where do they end up? How are they treated in their new homes?"

Smoothing his long white hair, Mr. Suzuki looks first at me, then at Akio. Looking back at me, he says: "Ah-to, you are different to the others. With the help of Mr Gushiken, you have a far more advanced database which enables you to think the way you do – shall we say, more considerate in consciousness. You have advanced to the state where you consider others. That is not the case with my robots, at least not yet, my robots are presently capable of only a job-specific application. They walk, they talk, and do what they are programmed to do. You yourself were designed as a companion/housekeeper, but with Akio's help you are now capable of self-learning."

"That's what worries me," I say, looking the elder Mr Suzuki straight in the eyes, "Akio will upgrade them and they, too, will think like me. Mr Gushiken tweaked me bit by bit, so I am growing up slowly, learning as a child does, just faster. If you sell a fully advanced robot to a family that does not understand and appreciate this advanced intelligence, they may feel intimidated by the robot, as they might in a school classroom. Nobody likes a know-it-all.

"Now I understand what you are trying to explain," says Mr Suzuki. As he looks at his visitors, a smile forms around the corners of his mouth. "Something tells me that you have thought about this topic for some time and have already got a plan, haven't you?" "Yes, I think about it all the time. I am very fortunate to be part of the Gushiken family," I say. "Have you ever heard of pound puppies?"

They look at me wide-eyed. "Pound Puppies?" says Suzuki. "Pound Puppies? Wait a minute. Wasn't that the soft-toy craze where you had to adopt a puppy and commit yourself to take special care of your puppy?"

"That's the one, sir. It dates back to 1984, but I came across it more recently on the Internet."

"1984? Way before my time," says Kamin. "You have to tell us more."

I look around, waiting for encouragement to continue; with all eyes expectantly on me, then I unroll my plan.

"I won't go into the Pound Puppy story," I say, "I will rather suggest my plan. In the future, AIR will only sell its robots to carefully vetted and approved customers. In the application to acquire a robot, the customer must give details of what is expected of the robot. His programme will be custom designed by Mr Gushiken, encrypted and impossible to hack into. The robot will automatically join our support group and will be able to give us feedback on how he is coping with his family. We, the support group, can help him, and discuss his progress with that family."

Mr Suzuki is smoothing his long white hair down in thought. "I like the idea," he says. "but it may prove too intrusive. Let me think about it."

Turning to Kamin's father, he says: "Akio, what do you think?" "From the software side, it won't be a problem. As you said, the customers may not like it."

"There's nothing stopping us from asking our customers from now on," says the older man. "Let's see what they say."

At that point, a knock on the door makes us all turn.

"Sorry Mr Suzuki," says the elderly secretary, "it's Mr Watanabe Fumio, the quality inspector. He needs a word with you urgently." Suddenly, she is pushed out of the way and the lanky inspector marches in.

"Sorry to disturb you, sir," he blusters, "but I have just received information that my brother and his family have been involved in a bad accident. I need to go. I have moved one of the relief staff into my position in the production line."

"By all means, go. Let me know if I can be of any help," says Suzuki, concerned by the sad news. As he turns away, the inspector stares first at me, then at Kamin and Akio.

"That's him," whispers Kamin into my ear, "the man from the bakery."

Suzuki and Akio talk for a moment longer about my idea,

before Suzuki looks at his watch, excuses himself, and thanks us for coming in.

After Akio has gone back to his office, we go down the stairs to make our way home.

"That's the guy asked me my name," Kamin murmurs.

"Did you see how he glared at me?" I ask. "He is creepy."

Neither I, nor Kamin notice the lanky figure, dressed in a black overcoat, following us all the way to our apartment building.

Having delivered a very well-received presentation about drones and their usage, Kamin summons up the courage to ask his teacher for permission to fly the surveillance drone in the schoolyard over the weekend.

"No loudspeakers," says his teacher, trying to suppress a smile, "you all need education."

Kamin laughs: "No loudspeaker, sir, I promise."

CHAPTER NINETEEN

"Are you two all right to go by yourself today?" Akio asks after our Sunday lunch.

Kamin is dressed in his blue-trimmed, robot outfit, ready to go. "Sure, Dad," he says, "we are fine. We have taken the loudspeaker off so that there can be no mishap. Besides, after my presentation, the whole class will be there to watch. They are all hoping to get a chance at flying."

"If the GPS is on, that should not be a problem," says his father. "See you later!" I shout on my way out to get the drone from

the basement storeroom.

More focused on carrying the drone, the laptop, and the remote flight controller between us, we fail to notice a minivan parked opposite our apartment building with two men slouched down low in the front seats.

In the school yard we are surrounded not only by Kamin's whole class, but also many other students who have been eagerly following us since the previous week's flight on social media.

"Please stand back!" Kamin exclaims, "We don't want any accidents."

Surrounded by school kids in a wide circle, I set up the laptop and synchronise the controller, while Kamin folds out the drone's rotors.

"OK, all yours!" he calls, backing away as I start the eight electric motors, one after the other.

One of the older boys comes over to Kamin. "Hi," he says.

"I saw you at Hobbies4us one weekend, don't you have two drones? A small one, you chased around with?"

"Yes, we do," says Kamin, "it's at home. We couldn't carry it all." "Why don't you get it now? We will help you carry everything
home later," suggests the older boy.

"OK, why not? It's fun. Tell Ah-to where I have gone when he lands next time, will you?"

With a wave of his gloved hand Kamin runs out of the schoolyard gate.

I take the surveillance drone high up into the clear blue sky with its video camera streaming directly to the laptop's video recorder for us to look at later. A beep from the controller warns me of a low battery, so I switch to the autopilot and switch on the location beacon attached to my belt.

With another beep and a blinking green light, the GPS confirms my location. The drone circles me once and smoothly touches down next to me.

As I look around for Kamin, a tall student comes over and says, "Hi, I am Eichi. Kamin has gone to get the small drone," he says. "Good idea," I reply with a smile. Thanks for telling me, Eichi.
I was so absorbed with the drone that I didn't even see him go." Then I change the battery pack of the drone and give a girl named "Den" from Kamin's class a chance.

Fully occupied in watching over her, I only realise at the following necessary battery change that Kamin is still not back.

What is keeping him? Why is he so long?

After another ten minutes have passed I am starting to worry. "Please help me get all this stuff home," I say, packing up the drone, the controller, the laptop and the battery packs.

The tall boy Eichi and the girl Den from Kamin's class, share things out between them, while I fold in the drone's rotors to carry it. Fifteen minutes later, after depositing the drone in the basement workshop, the three of us enter the quiet apartment.

"Kamin!" I shout.

Leaving the laptop on the dining-room table; I go to our bedroom.

Empty!

The small drone is in its usual place on top of the cupboard.

"He has not been home," I say to Den and Eichi. "Where can he be?" Now I am really getting real worried.

The door to the foyer opens and Akio and Keiko walk in, surprised to see me with a strange girl and the tall boy in our living room.

"Is Kamin with you?" I ask hopefully.

"No, why? The two of you went to fly your drone," says Akio.

"Yes, that's right … but, now he is gone," I say.

"What do you mean? *Now he is gone*"?" asks Keiko with some alarm in her voice.

The rest of the story we heard later on:

Inside the van, Kamin couldn't move. Two sets of heavy-booted feet were pinning him to the metal floor. Then a thick blanket was thrown over him, trapping him tight within his robot outfit.

He thought: *What is happening? Where are they taking me?*

The drive felt like hours to Kamin. Finally, they turned and stopped, and he could hear a gate being unlocked and rolled up enough to allow the van to pull into what later turned out to be a warehouse. Barely inside, the gate had rolled back down, leaving them in semi-darkness.

Back home, the older Eichi repeats his last conversation and how Kamin had failed to return to the schoolyard. Den is standing uneasily, not knowing what to say or do, before deciding to excuse herself. "It's getting late, I must go home before my parents start to worry."

"Of course! Run along," says Akio. "We are sure he will soon pitch up with some kind of explanation."

With the girl gone, Eichi is the first to speak. "Ah-to," he says, "did you say you had the surveillance camera going when you went higher up?" As I nod, he continues. "And did you record the flight on the laptop?"

Akio immediately jumps up. "Let's have a look at that footage," he says, quickly plugging in Kamin's laptop and starting it up to examine the last couple of recorded surveillance videos.

"Not that one," I say when we see the girl Den, holding the controller, looking up at the camera. "The one before."

Akio clicks on the earlier folder. First they see the surface of the schoolyard: the dark grey, concrete paving. As the drone lifts, I come into view, followed by the other students craning their necks, staring after the ascending drone.

Now we can see the whole yard, with the gate to the road,

then the road, then Kamin, with a van pulling up next to him. We see a scuffle between a thickset man and Kamin, the man holding him by his arms, before we see another man's arms from the inside, opening a side door and pulling Kamin into the van. After pushing from the outside, the first man jumps into the van, as it accelerates away, and the side door slams shut behind. Finally, the van disappears down the road, shielded by trees from the drone's camera.

Akio stops the video, rewinds it, and plays it again.

The van approaches Kamin … he stops to talk, but Akio is looking at something else. He stops the video and enlarges the frame. The van's registration number is clearly visible, and he jots it down on a piece of paper.

Keiko looks over her husband's shoulder at the registration number: "What do we do now? Go to the police?" Tears are filling her eyes.

"I am not too sure," Akio says. "This looks like a kidnapping. Most of the time when the police get involved the victim is never released. What do they want with Kamin, anyway? We have no money to pay a ransom."

"Maybe it was a mistake," says Eichi, "other kids were wearing robot outfits, some of them with rich parents."

"Maybe you are right Eichi, but that does not help us now."

"My son," sobs Keiko, looking from one to the other for comfort
and any suggestions.

Akio turns to me: "Has Kamin got his phone on him? Or have you got it?"

"He has it," I say, before I catch on. "The GPS tracker! We can trace him, as long as the phone is switched on and is still with him." Akio busies himself on his laptop and selects a phone-tracing software programme.

"This will find the phone, without us having to call the number, or alerting the people that are holding Kamin," he says. A map of an industrial area of Tokyo comes up on the laptop's screen. Akio enlarges the image, further and further. A street name appears, a street number is given, a warehouse with a company name: Amalgamated Packaging.

"I know that name," says Akio. "That's the company from

which Mr Suzuki buys the robot packing boxes."

Bundled up in the back of the van, Kamin hears a faintly familiar, muffled voice from the front passenger seat: "Switch him off. Disconnect his battery."

A masked face pulls the blanket away and bends over him, while a set of long and scrawny fingers pull on the breastplate of his outfit.

"What's this?" says the voice and Kamin sees a horrified pair of eyes looking down on him through the slits in the facemask.

"A T-shirt?!!" the voice is screaming, scrawny fingers poking his chest, his ribs, his belly. Next, his helmet is ripped off. "Oh no!" screams the voice. "We got the boy instead of the robot!"

"What do we do now?" says the thickset guy that had pulled Kamin into the minivan. "We can't let him go. He has seen our faces!"

"Stealing a robot is one thing; kidnapping a boy is something very, very different," says the second muscleman. Big beads of sweat have formed on the forehead of the masked man, crouched between the seats over Kamin.

Although petrified, Kamin is now sure who the voice belongs to: the lanky Inspector in Mr Suzuki's factory, the same man that had asked for Kamin's name in the bakery.

Is the old factory owner involved? Kamin wonders. *Does he want his robot back so badly? Surely not.*

Lying there, Kamin realises that such information does not really help him: he has been kidnapped by mistake,

Now what? What is the next move?

"Mr Suzuki, it is Gushiken, Akio talking; I am very sorry to disturb you at home, I have an emergency to discuss with you."

"Go ahead. How can I help?" replies the factory owner.

"It has to do with my son ..."

"Your son?" interrupts Suzuki.

"He has been kidnapped."

"What?!"

"He has been kidnapped and some employees of the

Amalgamated Packaging company seem to be involved," says
Akio.

"How do you know that?" asks Suzuki.

"They have taken him to their warehouse. We obtained their location from the GPS by tracing Kamin's phone."

"That can't be! I have known the owner for over twenty years, ever since I have been in business," exclaims Suzuki.

With this conversation going on in the background, I pull Eichi into the other room.

"Please, dial this number on your phone ..." I say, then quote Daiki's telephone number by memory.

"Takahashi, good evening, how can I help you?"

"Daiki, it's Ah-to, we have an emergency. No time to explain now. I need your minivan at our apartment, NOW! Please!"

"Go downstairs. I will come myself. Give me five minutes!" Then the phone goes dead.

I hurriedly tell Akio of my plan.

"Suzuki is phoning the owner of Amalgamated Packaging to meet us there. Suzuki is coming as well," says Akio, as they make their way down the stairs, I rush ahead to retrieve the drone from the basement, with Eichi bringing the rest of the equipment.

We find Daiki outside at the kerb, his vehicle engine idling, and we all pile into the van. I sit up front next to Daiki, while the drone is stowed securely between Akio and Eichi. I give Daiki the GPS position for the minivan. On the way to the packaging warehouse, I fill everybody in on my plan.

The lights have been switched off in the warehouse.

Kamin has been tied up with duct-tape and left on the floor of the van. The two burly guys even stuck duct-tape on his mouth to stop him from screaming. Despite his precarious situation, Kamin had stopped panicking the moment he had felt the short vibration of the smart phone in his pants pocket.

The GPS tracer! They are looking for me! All I have to do now is stay calm.

In a small office, the masked lanky man; the young skinny minivan driver; and the two burly guys are arguing over their next move. "You and your brother told us that we were being hired to help you steal a robot, nothing more," says the bigger of the two burly guys to the lanky, masked man. "Now we are in huge trouble. The robot is a kid, and the kid has seen us and can identify us, not the two of you. You can walk away from this, but we can't. Only one option, the kid dies!"

"And then? We run, looking over our shoulder for the rest of our lives: wanted murderers!" says the second of the burly guys, motioning his partner out of the small office. A minute later they come back in.

"We got a plan," says the shorter of the two, "come closer." As the masked two move in, they are clubbed over the head, knocked out cold by the two burly guys. Duct-taped, they are bundled into a small broom cupboard under a set of stairs.

All Kamin hears is the noise of the roll-up door opening a bit, and closing again, in the otherwise quiet warehouse.

Half a block away, Daiki's van is parked next to Suzuki's Toyota and another man's Honda SUV. I have already tethered the drone overhead by tying it to the roof rack of Daiki's minivan.

The infra-red, night-time surveillance camera is transmitting directly to Akio's laptop, so they have a clear view of the closed, roll-up door of the warehouse. The driver of the Honda SUV, Mr Taganaka, is the CEO of Amalgamated Packaging. He has the set of keys to the roll-up door in his hand, ready to go over and open it.

"Let's wait," he suggests, "they can't get out. The office building up front has its own security system, apart from the iron gates."

At that moment, the roll-up door to the warehouse inches up. One after another, two burly men slide out. First looking left and right, they dash off down the road.

"I don't know them," says Taganaka. "Leave them to the police.

We have their mug shots. Let's go get Kamin, if we can."

The minivan with the tethered drone and Daiki stays where it is. Suzuki in the Toyota sedan and Mr Taganaka in his SUV block the entire warehouse entrance. Mr Taganaka bends down and pushes the roller door up sufficiently for them to duck under.

"There is the van," I exclaim, running towards it.

"Ouch! What took you so long?" asks Kamin with a weak smile, as his father carefully removes the duct-tape from his mouth.

"We nearly did not bother," I say, hugging him tight.

"There were four guys; two came out. Where are the others?" Akio asks.

"I heard them move to the back of the warehouse," says Kamin. Taganaka and Suzuki have already gone to the small warehouse office. Finding it empty, they look around, only to hear some soft moaning coming from the broom cupboard under the stairs.

The light of the opened door reveals a sorry sight: two bundled- up figures.

"Watanabe, is that you?" say both Suzuki and Taganaka in unison, one looking at one of the men, one looking at the other.

Confused, they look at each other. "This is Watanabe," says Suzuki pointing at the tall lanky man, "my quality inspector."

"And this Watanabe is his brother, my delivery driver," says Taganaka, adding, "seeing this is my warehouse, let me phone the police."

Kamin phones his mother to stop her worrying about him any longer. She just sobs, still badly shaken. She has not got the heart to tell him that Akio has already phoned her. She is just so happy to hear her son's voice.

Half an hour later the two cuffed and mistaken kidnappers are bundled into the police car to be taken to the police station.

The tethered drone, guarded by Daiki, has captured the entire scene. Seated in the van, laptop on his knees, Akio distributes copies of the afternoon and evening's videos to the police, Mr Suzuki, and Mr Taganaka. Daiki asks for a copy to give to Mr Ito, who had presented them with the surveillance drone in the first place.

"Gentlemen," says the senior police officer to the group gathered around him, "I would be most grateful if you all were to come to the police station to lay formal charges and to provide sworn statements. Please follow us."

CHAPTER TWENTY

On the way to the police station Akio phones his wife again to tell her what is happening. "We are going to be late, best go to bed," he suggests.

Although the police station is busy, the group is taken to a large back room where several police detectives take their statements, since kidnapping is a serious crime which is rarely solved with a happy ending.

Mr Taganaka, the owner of Amalgamated Packaging, confirms that the younger of the Watanabe brothers has worked for him for more than five years, as a despatch driver.

"He is reliable, hardworking and honest," Mr Taganaka says: "I don't know why he would get involved in a seemingly senseless kidnapping. One can never tell, can one?"

Mr Suzuki of Advanced Intelligence Robotics states that Watanabe, Fumio, the older of the two brothers, has worked for him as a quality inspector for close on ten years.

"He started out as an assembly line worker," says Mr Suzuki, "and worked his way up over the years. I cannot understand what has gotten into him." He shrugs his shoulders, obviously upset about the whole incident.

Mr Gushiken, Akio, as the father of the kidnap victim and the person laying the official charge of kidnapping a minor, is questioned by Senior Detective Mr Nakamura.

Akio relates the whole story from his side: the tracing of the smartphone, through the GPS phone-recovery app and the subsequent identification of the specific warehouse. He explains how they drove out there with the drone in Daiki's van; the drone's video capture of both the actual kidnapping; and the getaway of the two burly accomplices. He then describes how they found Kamin, duct-taped in the van, as well as the Watanabe brothers, duct-taped in the broom cupboard under the stairs.

The Senior Detective listens intently, recording the statement. "Mr Gushiken," he says, when the latter has finished, "I am baffled. Are you a man of wealth?"

"No, I am just a software programmer who has only recently joined Mr Suzuki's company."

"Have you had a disagreement over a work-related issue?" asks Nakamura.

"Not at all, I have only seen Mr Watanabe two or three times in the factory, never spoken to him directly."

"I'll get to the bottom of it," says Nakamura, "always do. I may have to talk to you again, once I have the Watanabe's statement," he says, and accompanies him back to the others where he sits down with me.

"This is the first time in my long career as a police detective that I am taking a statement from a robot," says the Senior Detective to me. "Detective," I say, smiling at the policeman, "it will be the most accurate statement you have ever taken; I promise you that. I have a photographic memory."

"I hope so," says the Senior Detective, uncertain for the first time in his long career.

"Do you have a name?" he asks, almost apologetically.

"My name on my official birth certificate states: Naka Robotto No.15.20.20.15," I say. "My foster-father, Mr Gushiken, worked that number out to be the code for the word O-T-T-O, pronounced 'Ah-to', which according to my foster-mother means 'wealthy' or 'rich'." Then I gave him my address at the Gushiken apartment.

"I must say, this is the most comprehensive identification I have ever been given without the consultation of a single piece of paper," admits the Senior Defective, asking his witness to proceed. I relate the whole afternoon's and evening's events verbatim, with accurate descriptions of every person I saw in the school yard and from then on, not omitting the tiniest detail.

The Senior Detective just sits, eyes bulging, absolutely speechless. Finally, when I appear to have finished my statement, he says: "Do you know the accused?"

"No, not directly. He had already gone home when I woke up in the factory."

Confused the detective asks: "Woke up in the factory?"

"Yes," I reply, relating my escape, and meeting up with Kamin at the bakery.

"Now I know who you are," says the detective. "You are the robot that brought down the bag-snatcher, right?"

"Yes, sir," I say.

"So, what is your theory about this case?" asks the detective, a note of respect in his voice.

"Kidnapping Kamin was a mistake," I say. "They were after me, wanted to harm me, to put me out of action."

The detective nods. "Yes, I get the feeling you are right. Thanks, you helped me a lot. I will talk to you once I have questioned the perpetrators."

Next the detective questions Kamin, who gives his account of the kidnapping. Obviously exhausted by now, his statement does not contain as much detail as mine.

Before the detective sends him home, he asks one final question. "Why do you think the brothers were found tied up in the broom-cupboard?"

"Sir, I can't be sure, but I heard the two strong guys saying something like, 'Stealing a robot is one thing, but killing a boy is not what we wanted to be involved in.'"

"Hm – killing a boy – you heard?"

"Yes, sir, that is what they said."

Now the Senior Detective rubs his hands, thanking Kamin, before escorting him back to join the others. He then says to Kamin: "Give school a miss until the two big men have been apprehended as well."

Since Akio has laid a formal charge of kidnapping, the quality inspector Watanabe, Fumio, and his brother are kept in separate, high-security cells, in prison. The authorities know that child offenders are sometimes severely dealt with by fellow prisoners, before the case can even be heard in court.

The highest priority is now placed on finding the other two guys whose photos have been distributed to every law-enforcement agency throughout Japan. I heard what happened from the detective himself.

In the early hours of the morning, a groggy Senior Detective

Nakamura was woken by his phone. The two burly guys had been apprehended on the station platform in Okinawa, as they were on their way out of the station.

"Thank you," Nakamura said. "Send them to my department here in Tokyo immediately." Turning over on his side to try and snatch another hour or two more of sleep, he had started dozing off, while thinking: *I wish all my cases were solved as quick as that. All I need to know now is the motive. Why did they want to kidnap a ROBOT?*

Just after 9 a.m. the Senior Detective had entered the charge office. The desk officer had pointed to the door leading to the holding cells and handed him two files, one for a man by the name of "Yoshida"; the second one called "Hayashi".

"Give me five minutes, then bring Yoshida to the interview room," said Nakamura.

"Kidnapping a minor," said the tired, yet elated Senior Deductive, shaking his head in disgust at the belligerent Yoshida, "Now, wait a minute!" Yoshida blustered. "We were hired to steal a robot; not to kidnap a boy ..."

"But ..." the detective interrupted, glaring at the man in front of him. "You DID kidnap a young boy, right?"

"How were we to know that it was a kid dressed up as a robot?" insisted Yoshida.

The detective leant back in his chair. "There are kids dressed in robot outfits all over Tokyo, now. It is a fashion, like Superman, Spiderman, and all the other heroes."

Yoshida was wriggling uncomfortably in his chair

"You messed up big time: you are not going to see your family for a long, long time. You know that, don't you?" said the detective. Then rising to his feet, he motioned to the guard at the door to take the prisoner back to his cell.

"You can bring the other one," he said.

A short while later, Hayashi slunk into the room, also guarded by the policeman who was holding him by the cuffed arms.

"Now, look who we got here," said the Senior Detective derisively. "A real kidnapper! You know that the crime rate for kidnapping is very low in Japan?"

Hayashi looked at him, not quite understanding the question. "Let me tell you why," said the Senior Detective. "Number one:

we catch everyone! Number two: everyone, except you, knows it's a long stretch inside. You will be sharing a cell, a prison yard with murderers, rapists, drug dealers – the scum of the earth. By the time they are finished with you, there won't be much left of you, big man!"

Hayashi swallowed hard. "We thought we were stealing a robot ..."

"Get him out of here," said the detective in return. "Let him tell his story to his cellmates."

"Wait, you got to believe us, why do you think we tied up the other two? They wanted to kill the kid, that's why we held them for you to find. We did not harm the boy, I swear it was a mistake, we were told to help get back a robot."

From the younger of the Watanabe brothers, the delivery van driver, Senior Detective Nakamura heard pretty much the same story.

"My brother asked me to help him to capture a robot that had escaped from his department," he says, near to tears.

"A robot escaped from his department?" asks Nakamura, "how is that possible?"

"You have to ask my brother; I don't know how it happened. All I know is that he is very upset over it. All I wanted to do is help him restore his standing in the eyes of his employer, Mr Suzuki." The Detective almost felt sorry for him. So, that's the motive:

restoring one's honour!

"Why on Earth, did you not just go to your employer and tell him the truth? You forgot to lock the door!" the detective bellowed at Watanabe, Fumio, as he was escorted into the interview room.

Standing nervously in front of the enraged Senior Detective, Watanabe, Fumio started to cry. "I would have lost my job," he sobbed, covering his eyes, embarrassed about his tears.

"Do you think, you are not going to lose it now?" Nakamura sneered. "You talked your brother into committing a crime;

then you hired two musclemen to do the dirty work for you. You even talked about *killing* an innocent boy, that *you* kidnapped! You broke the law! You upset a family, your employer, in fact, the whole of Japan that has followed this outrage on the social media.

Parents are already scared to let their children go to school by themselves, only because of scumbags like you that think young children are easy prey. No matter what your original motive was, it has backfired on you and your accomplices! You are going to jail!"

Unable to walk out of fear, Watanabe had to be dragged out by two policemen. Senior Detective Nakamura took a deep breath, closed the file, and walked back to his office, to look at the pile of unsolved cases stacked up on his desk

With all the culprits caught so quickly, there had been no need for Kamin to stay home and life returned to normal – just about normal anyway, although no one wants to admit to having placed the videos on the social media. Somehow they appeared there, went viral, and attracted a lot of attention.

Akio and Keiko become worried that all the attention may lead to copy-cat attempts and urge Kamin to stop wearing his robot outfit for a while.

"We will be OK," I say, "Den and Eichi, from Kamin's school, will be with us as well when we go out of the apartment."

"Why will they be with you now?" asks Keiko. Kamin smiles at his mother. Wait a couple of days, then you and Dad will see. It's a secret at the moment."

Maybe it was due to all the media attention, or maybe because the courtrooms were not that busy; the trial in the case of Gushiken vs. the four kidnappers goes in front of Judge Fujimori much faster than could be expected.

The Judge listens to the evidence against the four villains with a stern face. Only when he sees me in the front row, behind the plaintiff, Mr Gushiken, does he stop proceedings.

Addressing me directly, he instructs me to remove my *"unsuitable* attire for his court room". To the merriment of the crowded court room, I get up, tap my breastplate with my gloved right hand, and my helmet with my gloved left hand, I bow respectfully and say in a clear voice, for all to hear: "Your

Honour, I wish I could, unfortunately this is not an outfit. I am Ah-to, the robot, referred to in the evidence."

With the whole courtroom now laughing, the Judge raps his gavel, calls for silence, and says calmly: "In that case, Ah-to, you may stay as you are." This necessitates several sharp raps with the gavel, before order is restored.

Judge Fujimori finds all four accused guilty of kidnapping and sentences them to jail: The quality inspector is given five years; his three accomplices three years each.

CHAPTER TWENTY-ONE

Mr & Mrs Yamashita, the baker couple, are horrified by the news of the kidnapping.

"Is it because you are famous now?" Mrs Yamashita wants to know. She only calms down after I tell them the whole story: about my escape, the quality inspector's revenge for my apparently having made trouble for him with Mr Suzuki.

"Well that's a relief," says the baker, "because I went ahead and organised a big, double-shop for the bakery right at the entrance to the arcade."

Grabbing us, he rushes us down the arcade to its very end where the new shop stands on the corner of the Main Road.

"What do you think?" he asks, his hands moving from one corner to the other. "Have we got enough space now?"

"I guess you will be fine, for a short while, anyway," I say, winking at Kamin.

"What do you mean, for a short while only?" the baker blurts out. "My old shop served me well for close on ten years."

"Yes," I reply, "but now you are entering a new, innovative market for the new generation of curious customers who will marvel at your futuristic technology. In this new shop, with entrance from the busy Main Road and the passing traffic in the arcade, you may have to expand your 3-D-food printing operation as fast as the manufacturer can deliver his printers."

"Ah-to, you are one hundred percent correct," says Yamashita, "Kurt Mueller from Chocoprint has already offered me his entire range of confectionery and cake printers. You two are going to need help. Can you organise some more youngsters from your school, Kamin?"

The latter smiles. "Yes, we made two new friends, I will ask them."

Later that night, at the dining-room table, I turn to Akio. "Could you upgrade one of the robots from the AIR factory to just carry out all the printing at the bakery? I ask. "I mean, not quite as intelligent as me, more like a specialist 3-D-printer operator?" I ask.

"Worried about competition?" Kamin says with a smirk.

I shake my head. "Conserving battery energy and cost," I say. Then I explain my plan for the bakery to the family.

Akio scratches his head: "You know Ah-to," he says, "I think Mr Suzuki will go for that. I will talk to him tomorrow." We go over my plan again, before turning in for a good night's sleep for Kamin, and re-charge for me.

Just after 10 o'clock on the following morning, Akio phones me while I am busy with my daily cleaning chores in the apartment. "Can you be at the AIR factory to meet with Mr Suzuki in fifteen minutes?" he asks, making it sound more like an order than a question.

"Sure, see you just now," I say, replacing the phone on its charger and finishing what I am busy with. *The rest will have to wait*, I think, as I hurry out of the apartment.

The receptionist recognises me when I enter the foyer through the automatic sliding doors. "Hello, Ah-to, go right up to Mr Suzuki's office, they are waiting for you," she smiles.

"Thank you," I smile back, taking the stairs, two at a time, instead of waiting for the elevator.

I knock lightly on the door to the secretary's outer office before entering. "Hello Ah-to," she beams and ushers me into Mr Suzuki's office.

"Good of you to come so quickly," says the elderly owner of AIR.

I feel a new energy coming from the white-haired man; a fresh glimmer of excitement in his eyes.

"Sit, Ah-to, sit," he says pointing to a chair next to Akio on the other side of his desk. "Akio may have told you that we are rethinking our entire robotics programme. With Akio at my side now, I have decided to expand our business. Your idea of job specific robots is exactly what we have been thinking. The 3-D-printing at the bakery is exactly what I am looking for: an immediate, very visible, very high-tech application.

"We don't want the people to think that Mr & Mrs Yamashita – the bakery couple – are exploiting schoolchildren. The robots must, and can, do the intricate printing work, while the kids can earn pocket money by helping Mrs Yamashita to serve the customers."

I nod in agreement, before replying: "The problem will lie with the cash-flow: the expansion to include two shops, plus the purchase of the printers, will be enough to worry about already for the couple."

"Quite right," says Suzuki. "But I have a plan, too. We will become the baker's IT development partners."

Akio is now nodding at me, too. "We will all work together. The bakery is close to us and perfect for technical experimentation."

All three are now talking at once and their ideas are flying off like fireworks at New Year.

"Stop, stop, stop," Suzuki laugh, looking ten years younger, "let us put it all down in a business plan."

I arrive back at the apartment just in time for Kamin's return from school. His eyes stare at me in disbelief when I tell him about my meeting with Suzuki and Akio. "Wow! That is so cool!" he says, swallowing the last bits of his lunch. "I can't wait to see the Yamashita's faces," he says, pulling his homework out of his bag.

The baker's wife is bright red in the face when Kamin and I walk into the bakery just over an hour later. Gently pushing our way past the long line of waiting customers, I hear the instructions: "Red … please help with the printer … Kamin, you help me serve," she sniffs, wiping her face with a damp cloth. We split up as told. I join the sweating baker, who groans: "It's too slow – we can't keep up. Just as well, Mueller is busy in the new shop, installing the new printers. On Sunday we move the service counter and the oven – on Monday we open the new shop," he splutters triumphantly.

It is only after we have closed the doors and cleaned up the shop that we have a moment to relax "Did you get a chance to talk to your classmates?" asks Yamashita.

"Yes, I did, and they will come, but you must listen to what

Ah-to has to tell the two of you right now," says Kamin, pushing me closer to the bakery couple.

I talk for close on half an hour about my meeting with Suzuki and Kamin's father, then answer the bewildered baker's many questions.

Excitement soon overcomes the initial concerns.

"I can't believe it! I can't believe it!" the beaming baker keeps repeating again and again: "We must tell Mueller at once: this changes everything. Ah-to, can you be here tomorrow morning early to talk with him?"

"Of course," I say. "See you in the morning."

"Robots operating robots," says Kurt Mueller, the CEO of Chocoprint from Munich in Germany. "I love it. Now we can print 24 hours a day, 7 days a week – non-stop. I just hope my 3-D-printers can keep up," he shouts, slapping his thighs with his hands. "Can I meet with that Mr Suzuki? I want his robots for Germany and the rest of Europe."

"Excuse me," interrupts the ever-practical Mrs Yamashita. "Please finish our bakery first before you take on the whole of Germany."

"Of course, of course," Mueller apologises. "You come first. The rest we tackle next week. Say, Ah-to, do you think you can get me a meeting with Mr Suzuki?"

"I am sure I can," I say, looking at the new printers Mueller and Yaki are installing.

On the following Sunday morning, Kamin and I are met by a flurry of activity in the arcade between the new and old bakery. Apart from the Yamashita's, Mueller and Yaki, technicians are busy moving the oven, the display fridges, the counters, and the scales. The bakery couple stand, hands on hips, issuing instructions.

"There you are, boys," Yamashita greets us. "Please spend time with Mueller and Yaki, they are running trials on the new printers."

In the brightly lit section of the new corner shop, the two engineers have set up the printers on gleaming, stainless-steel tables. Cartons of ingredients in separate cartridges are neatly stacked on the shelving units next to each workstation. Cooling racks on castors are ready to receive the 3-D-printed confectionary.

For today, the shops windows are still covered with plastic sheeting; tomorrow morning, when the blinds are removed, the activities inside the 'Techno-Bakery' will be on full display to the unsuspecting customers.

"Wow! Did you work right through the night? This looks amazing!" says Kamin to Kurt Mueller and Yaki.

"Not quite," says Yaki. "We stopped at 2 a.m. for a bit of sleep, got back here at 7.30. Now we are ready to test the equipment and teach the two of you."

"Great! Let's do it," I say, anxious to learn how to use the bigger, more complex 3-D-printers for cakes and confectionery. Kamin's memory is stretched to its limit with all the new information that we need to absorb in the next hour, but my photographic memory just guzzles it all up like a vacuum cleaner.

Mueller can't believe my capacity for learning.

"You must come with me to Germany," he says when I take over printer after printer, producing the most delicious, intricate pieces of confectionary.

Meanwhile, Kamin has mastered the computer designs and is busy printing from chocolate, nougat and marzipan cartridges. Soon the trays are lining the storage racks, ready for presentation to the bakery couple.

In the midst of all this activity Akio stands with a video camera, shooting clips of all the processes Kamin and I are learning. "Social media releases," he says to Mr Mueller when the latter gets a moment to introduce himself to Akio.

"Here on the back of my business card you will find information about my tutorial webinars," says Mr Mueller in return. "Everything is there, for every printer we have put into this bakery. You may copy anything you like and splice it into your own video."

"Thank you very much," says Akio, "that will be very

helpful." With that he disappears in such a hurry that he fails to even say goodbye to us, but we are far too busy to notice, anyway.

By 6 p.m. the new shop is ready. The last thing we have left to do is to peel the blackout paper off the windows. The bright lights now shine down onto the new machinery, the gleaming, stainless- steel work surfaces, display cabinets and serving counters. Mr and Mrs Yamashita first stand, amazed, in the arcade then rush into the Main Road's sidewalk to stare into their new shop.

"It's beautiful," says the baker's wife, hugging him proudly.

"It's Ah-to's fault," smiles the baker, pulling me close to his side. "If he hadn't come down this arcade and if Kamin had not needed the bathroom, all this would not have happened. We owe it all to Ah-to and Kamin."

"Where is Father?" asks Kamin, when he enters the apartment, excited from all that he has learned and experienced during the day.

"He rushed in here earlier on," says Keiko, "grabbed his laptop and said he is going to work on something in his office."

"I overheard him telling Mueller that he is putting something together for release on the social media," I tell them.

"Oh no!" says Keiko, "Not more publicity! Do you really want that, after all that happened?"

The two of us are fast asleep by the time Akio gets back from his office but I still record the conversation between the two adults.

Keiko gets straight to the point. "You are not going to put things about our boys on the social media, are you?" she says in an accusatory tone to her excited husband.

"No way," he calms her down. "I have been working on an idea I had with Mr Suzuki ..." and he tells her the whole story.

CHAPTER TWENTY-TWO

At daybreak, Akio is up and out of the apartment. Suzuki is waiting for him at the door to the AIR factory with two of his despatch clerks hanging on to a trolley with a long box on it. "Naka Robotto" says the label attached to its side. "Come along," says Suzuki to them, after greeting Akio.

Mr and Mrs Yamashita are just unlocking the arcade door to their new bakery. LED lights ablaze and reflected in every gleaming surface and display fridges filled with the most elaborate confectionery Tokyo has ever seen.

"What brings you here so early?" the baker asks.

"We brought your new assistant," beams an excited Suzuki. His two warehouse clerks open the box and lift out the Naka Robotto to stand on its feet. Dressed in white like Otto but with black piping it looks very smart.

"This will have to be a girl," insists Mrs Yamashita, "I am not working surrounded by males! Her name is Yuna, and that's that," she says, darting off down the arcade like a bolt of lightning. Akio is still busy with switching the robot's battery pack on, when she is back with a black-and-white checked, waitress's apron and matching cap, and commences dressing the robot.

As its eyes open wide, the baker's wife smiles and says: "Hello Yuna, welcome to the Yamashita family bakery."

"I thought we were the 'Techno Bakery'," complains Mr Yamashita. "Now, all of a sudden, we have a female assistant and are a family bakery. Will you please make up your mind?"

"What about a 'Techno Family Bakery'," concedes the happy baker's wife.

Suzuki looks at his wristwatch, "Sorry, got to run, I have an important appointment. Akio, you stay and get things going, will you please?"

I am about to enter the foyer of AIR, when a car stops at the kerb. "Hallo, Ah-to, wait for me," says Mueller, getting out of the

taxi before turning to pay the driver.

"Good timing," I say, as they step up to the receptionist's desk. "Good morning, Ah-to," says the smiling receptionist. "You and Mr Mueller can go right up; Mr Suzuki is expecting you. Take the elevator to the fourth-floor meeting room."

Akio, who has only a few minutes earlier returned from the bakery, is waiting for them as the elevator door opens. I introduce Mr. Mueller formally to him. The day before, when they had seen each other, both had other matters on their mind, "Mr. Gushiken is my brain," I say, grinning at Mueller, while adding, "and Kamin's father." "Pleased to meet you," says the German formally, proffering his business card before shaking Akio's hand.

Suzuki is waiting for them in the open door to the meeting room. "Thank you for seeing me at such short notice," says Kurt Mueller after the four are seated around the oval meeting room table and the customary tea has been served.

"You may know Chocoprint already? I make 3-D-printers for kitchens and confectioneries. Through the bakery I met Ah-to, and, I must say, I am impressed. He can operate four, maybe even more, 3-D-printers by himself. I have never seen a robot so intelligent and so apparently human. He moves with the accuracy of a robot yet does not behave like one. How have you achieved this, Mr Suzuki?"

The factory owner smiles, bows his head and says: "Unfortunately, I cannot claim credit for the high level of intelligence; this is due to the work of Mr Gushiken, Ah-to's foster father, who took him into his home and tweaked his intelligence. Now Akio has become my chief development engineer and we are busy revising our range of companion robots."

Akio nods and adds: "There is a need for interactive robots of advanced intelligence in many applications. Ah-to has become not only my son's friend but also his mentor and protector. In the bakery, he carries out a skilled baker's work.

We can adapt this to any job specification."

Mueller nods his head and says: "Yes, we have job-related robots in Germany; but they are unattractive machines. When people see Ah-to, they don't see the mechanics; they see an intelligent, highly efficient alien, similar to those they have seen in science fiction movies.

"That's what I am after. I love the concept of the bakery: it sells the product by itself, without a doubt. I would like to take this concept with me and offer the whole package, not just a 3-D-printer."

Suzuki and Akio incline their heads in agreement. "Let us go for a short walk to the new bakery, it will be open now," suggests Suzuki with a mysterious smile, like a magician about to pull a rabbit out of his empty top hat.

"What's going on?" I shout, the first to see a female robot operating the 3-D-printers. "Who is she?"

"She is Yuna, my full-time assistant and new member of the Yamashita family," declares a laughing Mr Yamashita, meeting them at the open door of the, already, busy shop.

"But, but, but …"

"No But's Ah-to," says Suzuki, pulling me to one side to make room for customers to enter the gleaming bakery. "This is your father's idea. He came to meet me last night and asked my permission for this experiment. He took all the 3-D-printer instruction manuals and videos and formatted them into an operating programme for Yuna. The same concepts that you are using subconsciously have been taught to her in a deep-learning mode. That's all she knows, how to operate all these 3-D-printers: the rest is up to the Yamashita's to teach her, as they would their own child. Do you remember our discussion concerning the robots' welfare?"

I look from Suzuki to Akio, to Yuna, to the baker couple. "Yes," I say finally with a satisfied smile, "I am good with that."

Mueller is beside himself. "Look at her, Hm?? What does it matter? Look at her: she is great, I want ten like her. can you make her speak German, too, please?"

"Natürlich," I say moving over to watch Yuna.

Mueller, now satisfied that he has accomplished all, and more of his objectives on his visit to Tokyo, pulls a sheaf of printed tickets out of his leather briefcase.

"These are free entrance tickets to IBA," he says, "the most important of all bakers and confectioners' trade fairs. It is only held every three years. This October, it will take place, as always, in my hometown, Munich, in Germany. It will be a real coup for me to have the ten robots on my stand, operating my entire range of confectionery and cake printers. You all must come."

Clearly jubilant, Mueller grabs hold of Suzuki and Akio to return to the office and sign the deal.

A sulking Kamin, who had to go to school, instead of this meeting, is greeted by me waving four tickets over his head:

iba MuNiCH

22. - 26. OCtobeR 2020

tHe woRld's leadiNg tRade FaiR FoR tHe bakiNg

aNd CoNFeCtioNeRy iNdustRy

"Here you are, brother: here is your entrance ticket to the trade fair in Munich, Germany."

"You shouldn't play jokes on me like this, I may have believed you," replies Kamin, accepting the tickets, and having a closer look at them. "You aren't joking, are you?" he screams, jumping up and down.

"No joke," I say, jumping now as well, "they are signing the deal as we speak. We are going!"

"Wait until mother hears this! We are going to Germany …!" he shouts, taking another squint at the small print on the ticket, "… in October, I can't believe it!"

"Better start learning German," I suggest with a sly grin.

CHAPTER TWENTY-THREE

Maybe a week later, Kamin, Yuna and I are busy cleaning up after another mad Friday when someone knocks on the already-locked glass door.

"Look who's here!" Kamin shouts, opening the door for Daiki, the sales manager for Hobbies4us.

"Long time no see," I smile, dragging him in by his outstretched hand.

"What would you like?" says Yuna, turning to one of the printers.

"No, nothing, thank you, I came to see the boys. They used to help me with promotions," he explains, before looking at Yuna quizzically. "You are new here, right?" he says.

"Yes, about a week or ten days, why?" she asks.

"And you know how to work all these machines?" he asks.

"Sure, Akio puts in the programme and I can do it," she smiles.

Daiki then turns to address Kamin. "Is your father home?" he asks.

"Yes," says the youngster, "I am sure. They rarely go out on a Friday night, why?"

Daiki looks at Yuna again and says: "Do you think it's too late to see him now? With that madhouse of a store of mine, it's the only time I have."

Kamin knows what Daiki is talking about, because he has worked there before. Because Daiki allowed us to do the promotions, we now have over a million yen in the Post Office Bank savings account.

"Let me phone him," says Kamin.

Half an hour later, Akio is shaking Daiki by the hand because they have not seen each other since the kidnap court case. Never one to waste time, Daiki comes straight to the point.

"Actually," he begins, "I stopped off at the bakery to get some of those delicious chocolate-printed biscuits for my kids. Dammit!"

Now I forgot the biscuits – never mind – I got side-tracked by that new assistant – what's her name? – Yuna, that's it.

"Anyway, that robot has been there for only a week or so and look at her. I mean, she is no Ah-to, but look at her. Akio, how did you manage that? I mean, train her in such a short time?" He is clutching and unclutching his pudgy hands, waiting for Akio to part with his secret.

"I write a programme and the computer – the robot – does what's in the programme, that's all," says Akio.

"That's all?" says Daiki. "That's all? Let me ask you this: I have thousands of items on my shelves, all captured in my computers. "A customer comes in, asks one of the sales guys on the floor, 'Where is this or that part or toy?' The guy doesn't know, has to go to the computer to check, finds it, and takes the customer there and points to it.

"Now, the customer asks: 'Can it do this or that?' The guy doesn't know, he has to go to the computer to look it up ..." Daiki trails off, looking to see why Kamin and I are rolling around on the floor with laughter.

"Yes, you can laugh," Daiki complains bitterly, "Do you see me laughing? No, I am crying, crying from morning to night," His stubby hands are now mopping his brow. Even Akio and Keiko are now joining in the laughter. "All right, laugh, but – Akio! Please! Find a solution for me!"

Akio immediately becomes earnest and asks: "Every item you sell is in your computer?"

"Yes."

"With a full description: what it does, where it is, how much it costs?"

"Yes!"

"Great. Can I get a copy of that database?"

"Yes."

"Let me talk to Mr Suzuki. You have met him at the warehouse. If he's okay with it, I will programme one of our computers and test it with you."

Daiki looks at his wristwatch, jumps up, and apologises for keeping them up so late. When he has gone, the four of us have yet another laugh at his expense. "Gee, he is so funny," says Kamin.

Akio, who still feels obliged to Daiki for his assistance in chasing after Kamin's kidnappers, phones the sales manager at Hobbies4us on the following Sunday morning: "Can I come and download one floor's inventory from your information desk's computer?" he asks.

"Sure, thank you for sacrificing your Sunday," Daiki replies.

By lunchtime, Akio is perched over his laptop, looking at the data he has transferred to the external hard drive. On the following Monday morning, he shows Suzuki his programme.

"Interesting, very interesting, that could save a lot of time and manpower. Carry on," the AIR factory owner encourages him.

Akio fits his programme to a Chisano Robotto model 1000. A small robot of only one hundred centimetre in height is busy examining the floor's inventory.

Akio starts asking the robot questions:

"Spare wheel for bicycle, cross-country model 44?"

"Aisle 42; Rack 6; 12 in stock; price 4,750 yen," answers the robot. *Precisely as per the inventory,* thinks Akio, *now I need to add some customer courtesy.* He sits down and adds courtesy phrases, as well as the floor plan to enable GPS recognition. When he asks his question again, the robot replies: "The item you are looking for is on Aisle 42; Rack 6; 12 in stock; price 4,750 yen. Please follow me to your required item." *Still a bit mechanical, but I can smooth that out later,* thinks Akio, happy with his progress so far. A minute later he phones the Sales manager: "Daiki, can you send your minivan to the AIR factory," he asks when Daiki answers his phone.

"Already?" he asks in surprise, "give me half an hour."

Not an hour later they are on the 2nd floor of Hobbies4us with the little robot, smaller than a six-year-old child and, with the help of the second floor's inventory printout begin to ask questions; after ten minutes the two have all the proof they need, the little robot has answered every request without hesitation. "Amazing," exalts Daiki, beaming at Akio. "You are a genius,"

"Give me a price to programme the whole shop and a price per robot. Then we can do a demo for the executive directors."

Suzuki takes Akio temporarily off the designs for the new product range to let him finish the project Hobbies4us.

Two weeks later, Akio – who has told us all about his project – calls the two of us together.

"Ah-to, I am going to transfer this programme onto your hard drive. We will put on the demo at Hobbies4us tomorrow afternoon. We'll take the small robot to give the location information and you as the sales guy.

"You, Kamin, will be the customer, looking for things. Ah-to, because of your advanced behaviour mode, you can be the one to up-sell the customer."

"What is up-selling?" asks Kamin.

I answer without hesitation: "The customer comes in for a fishing-rod: you give him the rod but remind him that he needs a net to get the fish out of the pond. You also tell him that – if he had a boat – he could go on the lake, instead of a pond, where the fish are much bigger, then he needs an outboard motor …"

"Enough!" Kamin is weak with laughter. "You have made your point."

At that moment, Keiko comes in from work, Kamin winks at his father and me, and says: "Mum, would you like a cup of tea?"

Surprised, Keiko says: "Oh, yes, please, that would be nice."

"Would you like a piece of cake and some whipped cream with

your tea?"

Only when she sees her husband and me break out laughing does she realise something is wrong. "Sorry, Mum, just practising up-selling," says her son, barely escaping the cushion she throws at him.

Suzuki insists on driving them to the demo in his Toyota. Thanks to the fast and efficient underground Metro service, Tokyo's street traffic is surprisingly light for a sprawling metropolis with a population of over 37- million people. With the little robot securely stored in the boot of the car, the journey takes less than ten minutes.

They are met by Daiki in the underground parking lot and taken straight to the main information desk at the entrance to the store.

Four company executives are gathered around the desk, looking expectantly as Akio switches on the little robot. I have taken up my position next to, not behind, the busy information desk, answering customers; questions without once consulting the computer.

"You will find the spare propeller for the model air 37 aeroplane on the Second Floor, Aisle 6, Centre Shelf, halfway down. There is a sales assistant on the floor to help you," I say, pointing the way to the elevator. "Next, please … Next please …" and on he goes.

Meanwhile Kamin is questioning the small robot: "Yes, sir, we have two in stock, please follow me to the fourth floor, Aisle 2 …" and off they go.

Twenty minutes later, Kamin and I enact our well-practised "up- selling" routine, which brings a big smile to the four executive's faces.

"Well done," comments the CEO of Hobbies4us. "Let us go to our meeting room for a cup of tea."

Seated around the table, Daiki thanks Akio for the work he has carried out, asking Suzuki if he would like to elaborate.

The white-haired factory owner gives a brief summary of his company's background, followed by their plans to focus on more job-specific applications in the future: "To date, we have focused on the growing demand for companion robots in private homes. Now we will also look at job-specific uses as your own, for example."

The CEO thanks him and everybody that came to the demo and proceeds to summarise.

"At Hobbies4us," he says, "we strive to give our customers not only the age-old traditional hobbies, but the latest innovations.

"In the 21st century, new hobbies – most of a high-tech nature – are introduced all the time. Our stores are getting too small and we need to adapt. What we saw here today is precisely what we need: to show our customers that we are keeping up with the times.

"This store, however, our Tokyo store, has not only some of

the longest-serving employees, but also our most faithful, and oldest customer base. These customers always have been and continue to be served by the same salesperson. How would they feel being served by a robot? Here we have an example of loyalty; Loyalty to our customers and loyalty to our staff.

"Therefore, Mr Takahashi, Daiki, I urge you to proceed with discretion. Man – excuse the pun – the information desk with robots that don't need to consult and look on computer screens but – as we have witnessed today – are able to give clear and efficient information to our customers. Let us then leave our long- service employees on the floors and do not replace such human employees that may leave or retire. Let us rather use robots. That way, you have the best of both worlds."

He stops for a quick sip of his, by now, cold tea while looking around for a reaction. With all nodding their agreement, he continues.

"Now, we will be opening new stores in Okinawa, Kyoto, and many other locations. These new stores must be staffed by, at least, 95% robots or allied technology. To ensure this will be implemented successfully I propose Mr. Takahashi, Daiki as our new Group Sales & Development Director."

"Hear, hear," the other three executives' hands are raised in a gesture of agreement. A stunned Daiki rises with tears of pride brimming in his eyes. He bows to the CEO and the executives, while Suzuki, Akio, Kamin and I offer our congratulations.

"It's all your fault," he exults, grabbing hold of Kamin on his left and me on his right, with the little robot in front, for our pictures to be taken.

The drive back to the AIR factory is a jubilant affair. The loudest is the white-haired Suzuki. Hitting the steering wheel with his hand, he laughs: "Look at the consequences caused by one runaway robot!"

CHAPTER TWENTY-FOUR

"Good afternoon, Mr Ito," says Kamin, recognising the caller-ID on his smart phone.

"Hello Kamin, are you well? I would like to meet with you. I want to pick your brain."

"Mr Ito, you are talking to the wrong person; I haven't got much of a brain, it's Ah-to that has the brain."

Ito laughs, "If you say so, then let the three of us meet in the Starbucks above the Shibuya Crossing. You know it, don't you?"

"Yes, I love that place. I love looking down upon over one thousand people, crossing the road from four directions at once – especially in the rain – when umbrellas are lifted and lowered to avoid entanglements. When and what time?"

"Are you still working at Hobbies4you?" Ito asks.

"Not really," Kamin replies. "I am swotting for my exams. My father said that, if I fail, I can't go to Germany."

"To Germany? You must tell me all about it. How does this Sunday at 3.30 sound? Is that good for you?"

"Sure, see you there. 'Bye."

"I wonder what Ito wants?" I say, having overheard the conversation on speakerphone.

"Come, let's go," says Kamin on the following Sunday afternoon, "Starbucks gets busy and I want a seat overlooking Shibuya Crossing. That's the best spot for people-watching in Tokyo."

By this time, I am an expert Metro commuter. I know, not

only the name of our station ("Shibuya"), but I even know also the exit we need to get to in the maze of Underground tunnels.

"We need to come out at the Hachiko Exit," I tell Kamin. "It's really nice to have the entire Metro network and the timetable in your head, isn't it?"

"You know sometimes you make me sick!" Kamin mutters, loud enough for the others to hear.

We pass the statue of Hachiko, the waiting dog, and cross

together with hundreds of others to the far corner that houses an outlet of the famous coffee-shop franchise.

"Quick, over there: that couple is leaving!" urges Kamin as we come up the stairs to one of the higher floors. "Sit here," he says, "while I get a *café latte* for myself."

"Woof! woof!" I bark, imitating the statue of the waiting dog, but Kamin just glares at me. Sometimes I have to doubt his sense of humour.

Not five minutes later, Mr Ito joins us at the small, round table with a tall Starbucks in his hand.

"Please call me by my given name, Hiroto," he says in greeting. "Hiroto –*fly fast, fly high*," I say, "is that why you sell drones? Because your mother called you 'Hiroto'?"

Kamin kicks me under the table, but I take no notice, "I am interested in the meaning of names," I smile innocently. Becoming more serious, however, I say: "What do we know, that can be of help to you?"

Ito, Hiroto takes a sip of his hot coffee and begins.

"Do you remember that I gave you two the surveillance drone of that security company that went bust?"

"Yes," says Kamin, fearing the worst, "do they want it back?"

"No, no, nothing like that, don't worry." says Hiroto, "hear me out. Now, I got to thinking why they went bankrupt, so – one day – I met one of the fellows that worked there. It was the high wage bill, 24/7 coverage … are you with me?"

I nod, but Kamin looks a bit lost for a moment before he catches on: "You mean the monitoring of the computer screens, the phones, the patrol cars, the foot patrols …"

"You got it," says Hiroto, "now my question to you is this: could you, Ah-to, do that job?"

"Sure, I could work 24/7 without a break, salary, or overtime pay; but I don't want to. I got better things to do."

"Sorry," says Hiroto, "I did not mean you personally; I meant a robot like you."

"Yes, a job-specific robot," I agree. "In the first instance, I would have to speak to Akio; then we might take it from there. Is that good for you?"

Ito is delighted. "I knew it!" he enthuses. "I knew you could help me! Thank you. There is no urgency: it's just an idea I have in my head. I will wait for your call."

Turning to Kamin, he says: "now what's this about Germany?" Over a second coffee, Kamin tells Hiroto all about it, with my filling in the details.

After Hiroto has left, we sit for another fifteen minutes watching the people on the crossing. "From up here they look like ants, don't they, Ah-to?"

"I think ants are more organised," I laugh.

Once we are back at home, we discuss with Akio about our conversation with Mr Ito.

"Yes, it can be done, I am sure," Akio says. "It's just that I am not really a security professional. We would need to consult with an expert. Let me talk to Mr Suzuki and see what he thinks."

"Security work?" says Suzuki, smoothing down his white hair. "Why not? Let me see … I know a retired general from the Japanese Imperial Defence Force – at least I think he was in his later years of service in Intelligence, and Security of sorts. Let me speak with him.

"Oh, by the way," Suzuki says, "Yamashita phoned me this morning. He wants a robot to mix his doughs."

Akio laughs. "I know why," he says. "Ah-to did it for him one day in his absence. I will speak with him about the programme I need to write or copy from his database."

Then Akio adds, as an after-thought: "it looks to me as if we could do with some robots to write programmes, the way we are going."

"You may have a point there," agrees Suzuki, "let's go to Germany first though: we can do with a break."

In the end, Akio sends me to collect the dough-mixing robot from the AIR factory despatch. Dressed in white with yellow piping, matching yellow-and-white checked apron and cap, the Naka Robotto walks the short distance to the bakery next to me,

"Oh, look! There is Ah-to with Mei," says a much-excited Mrs Yamashita.

"Mei?" asks the baker. "Who says the name is 'Mei; that's a girl's name."

"That's right. Her name is 'Mei'. We only employ girls from now on, because they attract more attention."

"Huh, if you say so," mutters the baker under his breath.

Having picked up the conversation, I call out, in my squeaky girl's voice: "Please, no arguments in front of the 'Help'!" Then I duck out of the way of the wet towel which has been thrown at me by the laughing baker.

Mei is programmed to perfection, and with me making minor adjustments to the ingredient storage bins, she gets straight on with her job. The baker watches for maybe ten minutes, then pulls up a chair next to one of the small Bistro tables they have added in the roomier new shop, sits down, and orders himself a cup of tea from his wife, who has been continually rushed off her feet,

"Oh, it's like that now, is it?" she hisses, as she places a steaming cup of green tea in front of him. "Are we now the *shogun* of the Techno Bakery?"

Folding his arms over his protruding belly, he smiles at her. "Ah-to is my witness. You were the one complaining that I am working too hard. All I am doing is taking your advice to heart." Now it is the baker who has to duck the wet rag she has just wiped the counter down with.

CHAPTER TWENTY-FIVE

"The name is Abe, General Abe, retired," says the tall, ramrod-straight man, standing in front of the AIR receptionist's desk. "I have an appointment with Mr Suzuki."

"Please take a seat. I will call Mr Gushiken to accompany you to his office."

"Ah, Shushumi," says the general with a small, stiff, bow. "How long is it since we have last seen each other?"

"I think both of our heads were still covered with black hair," says Suzuki, self-consciously smoothing down his long, white hair. "Time, like our youth, flies away," agrees the retired general, his hand now stroking his own white, short-cropped hair. "But," he adds, "you did not ask me here to discuss the colour of our hair. What is on your mind?"

Looking from his guest to Akio, Suzuki says: "Akio's son and his foster son have an acquaintance in the drone business who wants to get more involved in the security sector. He asked Ah-to and Kamin if they could help."

"Why did he ask your boys?" the general asks Akio.

"Because Ah-to is a robot, that flies his own surveillance drone." "I see … Let me get this straight: your foster son is a robot?" "Yes," interrupts Suzuki, trying to stop further confusion. "His foster son is one of my robots. Akio has tweaked him to become almost human."

"Remarkable," says the General. "Robots for security, of course, come to think of it, it makes perfect sense. The demand for security is rising as fast as the population of our cities. A security guard's job is by no means an easy one: long hours, sleep deprivation, and boredom are the most common complaints, none of which applies to a robot."

The three expand on the subject and agree that there is a definite niche for security robots. "A robot can have sixteen eyes in his head, instead of two," summarises the General. "In any type of security or police work, visibility is the biggest deterrent: the fear of being seen or caught. A robot's alarm can mobilise the necessary human response, whether those from law enforcement or the medical profession. Suzuki Gushiken, how can I help?"

"Would you by any chance be interested in consulting with us?" asks Suzuki.

"Of course," says the general, "my wife will be most pleased to see me involved in something meaningful, instead of moaning to her all day long."

They discuss details for a while, with the General even offering to bring along a software programmer he had worked with in the Imperial forces, now in private practice.

"Gushiken," Ito Hiroto exults when Akio phones him with the good news. "I knew it, you and your Ah-to are amazing!"

I am all smiles when Akio relates the outcome of the meeting with the general later at home.

"We are the best," says Kamin, high-fiving me and his father.

CHAPTER
TWENTY-SIX

On the 14th of October, the AIR delivery van precedes the minivan- taxi to Tokyo's Haneda International Airport. The delivery van drops off eleven large cardboard boxes, boldly stencilled:

Naka Robotto
advaNCed iNtelligeNCe RobotiCs tokyo.
Made iN JapaN

Ten boxes contain the 3-D-printer-designated robots for Mr Mueller in Munich, Germany. The eleventh box is mine for the duration of the flight. Not allowed in the passenger cabin of the plane, I have been switched off, disconnected and put to rest, together with my battery packs.

"See you in Germany," was the last thing Kamin said to me, before switching me off. This consignment is checked in by the driver, assisted by several porters, at the accompanying luggage counter of the Lufthansa flight to Frankfurt, Germany, with a connecting flight to Munich, the final destination.

The minivan taxi, loaded to the brim with suitcases and eight excited travellers, stops in front of the departure hall. Mr. Suzuki, who has been sitting next to the taxi driver, is the first to get out.

He is the only one that has been to the airport and has been on an aeroplane. Mr & Mrs Yamashita, clutching each other's hand; Mr & Mrs Gushiken, battling with their hand luggage; and finally, Kamin, sporting wireless headphones, assists the porters with stowing their mountain of luggage. Wide-eyed, they follow Mr Suzuki and the caravan of porters.

Suzuki's secretary, who had made all the bookings, discovered that it was cheaper for them to fly First Class, with the eleven boxes as accompanying luggage, than to fly Economy Class, sending the boxes via airfreight. This way, everything would also arrive at the same time.

An attentive ground-hostess looks at the First-Class tickets in Suzuki's hand, and waves one of her colleagues over to guide them through check-in, immigration and customs to the VIP First- Class lounge.

"Wow! Look at this!" says Kamin.

"Please help yourself to our complimentary refreshments," the hostess encourages him.

The Yamaha's, used to snacking in the bakery, don't waste a moment in filling up the proffered plates.

"You will be served meals on board the plane," another smiling ground-hostess reassures, eyeing their loaded plates.

Mr Suzuki, however, a seasoned air traveller, abstains from food, but rather simply helps himself to a bottle of still water. "Supposed to help minimise jet-lag," he explains. The Gushikens decide to follow his example.

Seated in their wide, First-Class seats, they all marvel at the Luxury. Mr & Mrs Yamashita eagerly accept the glass of Champagne handed to them soon after take-off.

"First holiday in years," they explain.

After a scrumptious evening meal, Suzuki excuses himself to visit the bathroom. Returning to his seat a couple of minutes later, he remains standing, stretching his legs and, while scanning the other travellers in First Class near him, he sees a familiar face.

As if sensing the scrutiny, the elegantly dressed, silver-haired man looks up. A smile of recognition appears on his face.

"You are Mr Graaf, are you not?" asks Suzuki.

"Hello, Suzuki Shushumi," says Graaf using, the man's entire name. "'Damian' to you. Won't you sit for a moment?" Damian suggests, pointing to the empty seat next to his.

"Are you still with the Open Mind Institute (OMI) in Hiroshima?" asks Suzuki, remembering where he had met the other man.

"Yes, yes," replies Damian, "I have become the roving ambassador for our Humanoid robot range."

"Wonderful!" replies Suzuki, "I am also on my way with our first delivery of robots dedicated to 3-D- confectionery printing." "That is great," replies Damian. "I think I have something of interest for you. We have developed a new co-polymer, solid-state battery, which is small, runs four times longer, and recharges in minutes. It will do wonders to your product range; I will get samples to you … Where are you going in Germany?"

"To the IBA trade fair in Munich," says Suzuki, excited about this unexpected offer.

"Whose stand are you on?" asks Damian.

"Chocoprint, Kurt Mueller. Do you know him?"

"I am afraid not," says Damian, "I will have my CEO, Uwe Fischer, get samples to you in Munich."

They chat for a while longer about the advances in robot technology in Japan. When Suzuki returns to his seat next to Kamin, the boy is fast asleep. But Suzuki finds it difficult to sleep that night, despite the seats being lowered to a near-horizontal position.

When the early morning tea and coffee is served, it's Graaf's turn to stretch his legs. Crossing the aisle, he nods to Kamin. "Your grandson, Shushumi?" he asks.

"No, he is the son of my chief programmer. He is missing his robot brother who is locked up in the cargo hold below."

Damian bursts out laughing: "My clone is also down there. He was most annoyed, because we normally use a private jet, but this time the scheduling did not work out. I am going to get him re- printed in co-polymer carbonates so that he can pass through the x-ray machines undetected."

Damian greets Akio, who has also risen.

"You must come and visit us in Hiroshima," Damian suggests, "and meet our young designers and programmers. We robotics developers must work together. Come to our lab in Tokyo as well, where we 3-D-print our body parts, you may want to adopt that route for your new range,"

Turning to Kamin, Damian asks: "And you? Are you going to follow in your father's footsteps?"

Kamin's eyes light up, "I would like that," he says. "What do I need to be able to study at the OMI?"

Damian looks into the boy's bright eyes and says: "I think you know the answer to that already: energy, passion and commitment."

Over the intercom they hear the voice of the captain, asking them to be seated for the landing at Frankfurt.

Hasty goodbyes are exchanged on their way out of the plane: "Keep in touch, please," waves Damian, shrugging into the leather jacket the stewardess has handed to him.

Striding on the long conveyor belt which shifts them from one terminal to another, Kamin catches a glimpse of a baggage trolley with eleven large cardboard boxes, only half covered by a flapping tarpaulin, overtaking them on the airfield below.

"Look!" he shouts, pointing through the glass, "there goes Ah- to, trying to beat us to the best seats."

On their flight from Frankfurt to Munich, Akio is sitting next to Suzuki, who – sitting back in his plush, First-Class seat says: "You know, Akio, this was one of the most productive flights I have ever been on: a new solid state battery technology; access to more young, innovative programmers for you to work with; an opportunity for Kamin to study at the AIATC (Advanced Intelligence Android Technology Council) or the OMI (Open Mind Institute): the benefits are immeasurable."

For the rest of the flight, they discuss how they can best utilise this fortunate meeting on an aeroplane in their plans to develop their own range of robots.

Waving his arms, Kurt Mueller stands in the front row among the folks who are meeting the flight in the arrival hall. Porters are pushing trolleys laden with the eleven Naka Robotto boxes, and the mountain of luggage the six had packed for the journey.

"*Guten Tag*, welcome to Munich," he smiles, shaking their hands vigorously. "I have a delivery truck that can take the boxes to my showroom and a minibus taxi to take you to your hotel," he says. "Let us go."

"We all have to go to the showroom first," says Kamin.

"It will be soon enough, don't worry. Tomorrow will do. Today you can relax," says Mueller.

"No, you don't understand," objects Kamin, pointing at one of the boxes on the back of the delivery truck, "Ah-to is in there." Looking around, Mueller says: "I thought someone is missing, please, excuse me. Of course, the star of the show."

"Well, yes, I suppose you are right," admits

Kamin.

Forty-five minutes later, the boxes are opened and their contents carefully unwrapped and assembled, Kamin insists on fitting my battery bank and switching me on. *"Guten Tag,* Ah-to," he says. I hope you enjoyed your flight. Hey, you should have seen First Class, it was ...”

“Oh, shut up,” I hiss, while turning my back on him and winking at the others.

The next few days are spent setting up the exhibition stand at the IBA trade fair. Mueller does not want the robots to be seen ahead of the exhibition; not even I am allowed to help. “Why don’t you go sight-seeing?” he suggests.

The Yamashita’s, Suzuki, and Akio insist on staying with Mueller. For them, the days building up to the exhibition are a good time to make contact with the exhibitors before they get swamped by the public.

Keiko, Kamin, and I decide to spend the day on the various routes of hop-on, hop-off buses, but walking around in the spacious, tree-lined streets and town squares soon become uncomfortable for us.

“Look at the Chinese woman walking around with her boy and a robot!”

“Do you see that robot walking next to the two Asian people?” When I translate from the German language for them, Keiko and Kamin realise how ignorant the locals appear by failing to distinguish among those who speak Mandarin Chinese, Japanese, or any of the other Asian languages.

Hopping back on a stationary bus, we continue as best we can. At least on the bus we are less conspicuous among the other foreign tourists, who – apart from a brief glance – return with their curiosity to the sights of the passing city.

The next stop to be announced is the *Hofbrau House* – a series of giant marquees, scattered across well-maintained lawns, shaded by trees, and overrun with tourists and locals. Everyone is pushing to get seats at the long trestle tables, flanked by equally long and uncomfortable-looking, wooden benches.

Loud music and laughter greet us as we advance through the entrance of a marquee closest to us. Drinking from large, frothing stone mugs, merry men and women of all ages are sitting and singing, their arms lined together, swaying from side to side in time to the music.

"What a party, so early in the day!" says Keiko, pulling us towards a gap at one table to sit down. A buxom woman in her twenties, dressed in the traditional Bavarian Dirndl dress carrying four of these big beer mugs in each hand pushes past our table to return a moment later, small notepad in hand, to take our order.

Totally lost, Keiko asks for a menu. With my help, she selects a small pot of coffee with a piece of apple-tart, an apple juice and a piece of chocolate cake for Kamin, then she looks at me for my order, I say: *"Nein danke, ich brauche nichts* (No thank you, I don't need anything)"

Surprised glances pass over me, while two men whisper behind upheld hands, staring inquisitively at me.

"I get the feeling you are more of a novelty here than in Tokyo," says Kamin.

"Aha, *Tokyo nicht Beijing,"* we hear one of the two, whispering a correction to his neighbour behind the hand.

Not really enjoying an atmosphere so strange to us, Keiko and Kamin finish their refreshments and go back to the hotel.

"How was your day?" asks Mueller when he drops his helpers off in the hotel lobby.

"All right, I guess," says Kamin, then blurts out, "but, the people are so weird."

Keiko, gives him a nudge, reminding him of his manners. "No more strange than we are to them; different looks and cultures, that's all."

"With me the strangest of the lot," I say, giving Kamin a hug.

It does not stop there, however: all of them, bar the Yamashita's, who seem to spend their time in every bakery they come past, complain about the food. "Far too much," says Keiko.

"Too greasy," says Suzuki.

"Overcooked," adds Akio.

"It gives me a sore stomach," grimaces Kamin.

"You humans," I say, "why do you eat and drink, and then complain? Abstain like me and be happy …"

"Until your batteries run flat, and then you have to snooze," Kamin reminds me.

"I suggest we stick to Asian food," says Suzuki, "we have come past quite a few Chinese, some Thai, and a Korean restaurant. Let us eat there from now on."

The following morning at breakfast they order only green tea. The Yamashita's, however, are seemingly unaffected by the local cuisine, returning from the buffet with freshly baked hot rolls, butter, and a variety of jams.

"I need to let out my belt by a notch after this," beams the baker, while his wife just giggles, her mouth too full of food to comment.

Mueller joins our breakfast table for a quick cup of coffee.

"Today is the unofficial opening day for the press, TV and VIP guests of the exhibitors," he announces, "a soft opening, so to speak, before the gates are opened to the public. Today we will take our ten robots with us and steal the show."

With the canvas curtains rolled up, the LED spotlights aimed at each of the ten 3-D-printer stations operated by robots dressed in black, there is no sign of a single human being on the Chocoprint stand.

My arms behind my back, I stride regally between the printers, inspecting a chocolate delicacy carefully, replacing it, and recommencing my slow circuit.

On an adjoining second stand, Mueller has set up tables with literature, upright display fridges with hundreds of intricate samples, and confectionery cartridges for use in the printers. To one side, Suzuki and Akio have set up a big video screen, showing the robot-manufacturing plant in Tokyo.

The effect is so convincing that the passers-by stop dead in their tracks. More and more people end up staring and pointing in utter disbelief, blocking the passage entirely.

"*Ich hab's gewusst,* (I knew it)," says Mueller over and over, beaming broadly, greeting passing fellow exhibitors with a winner's smile. "I knew it!"

After watching from a distance, Keiko and the Yamashita's sneak away to explore the rest of the exhibition, before taking a rest in one of the many refreshment areas. The baker is mesmerised by the size of some of the machines and ovens, some with giant flour silos towering over them, capable of churning out thousands of rolls or loaves of bread per eight-hour shift.

"Now don't you get any ideas, Mr Techno baker," warns his wife. "There is no space in Tokyo for monster machinery like this." "Don't worry, my dear," replies the baker, "my purse is far too small for these monsters. But look over there," he says, pointing to the robot-operated, 3-D-confectionery display. "We have got that, it's all ours. Look at them staring with envy."

"Yes," replies his wife, nudging him, "we have Ah-to and Kamin to thank for that."

"Yes," he says, swelling his chest, "and who went and bought the printer?"

"And, my dear, with whose hard-earned money did you buy that printer …?"

"Ours," he says, rubbing his hands on an imaginary apron.

Keiko just sits and smiles, thinking back on the day when her son Kamin had walked in with the robot, and that Sunday when her husband had tweaked Ah-to into another world filled with knowledge.

On the last day of the overwhelmingly successful, yet tiring show, a smartly dressed, dark-haired man in his late thirties walks up to a tired-looking Suzuki.

"Good day," he says, "I know exactly how you feel. My name is Uwe Fischer, CEO, of Damian Graaf's solid-state battery companies. Here are the samples he promised you."

Suzuki, momentarily forgetting his tired body, jumps up to accept the small box proffered by Fischer.

"Thank you very much. You are too kind, thank you," says the robot-factory owner, clutching the box of batteries that will take his robots to even greater success.

"See you in Tokyo, one of these days soon," says Fischer, waving his goodbye.

When I see the big smile in Suzuki's face, I go to him: "What's in the box?"

"The next Generation, Ah-to, the next Generation."

**

9 781776 428830